***Kyle knew he should disengage himself from her.***

Knew that he should say something about being her superior on this case and that they had a professional relationship to maintain. They were coworkers, and these kinds of things—even if it was only a one-time thing—rarely, if ever, worked out. He wasn't in the market for a relationship, and a one-night stand with a fellow detective just wasn't a good idea.

But for the life of him, he couldn't voice a single protest, couldn't put a single thought into words. He was only aware of the overwhelming desire that beat like the wings of a hummingbird within him. A desire that was growing by the second.

He wanted her.

Dear Reader,

Welcome back to the Cavanaugh clan. This time around,
the story is about an outsider, one of the triplets fathered
by Mike Cavanaugh. Admittedly, Kyle O'Brien has a large
chip on his shoulder. Until his mother's deathbed confession
rocked his world, Kyle thought his late father had been
a war hero. To discover that he and his siblings were the
product of an affair that ended badly placed his very identity
in jeopardy. Being welcomed into the family complicated
his mental dilemma.

But finding his place in the new scheme of things takes
second place to two events. One is that citizens are being
preyed upon by a serial killer who sees himself as a vampire
slayer. The other is that he is partnered with a woman who
brings a different kind of turmoil into his world, causing
Kyle to once again redefine himself and the world he
thought he inhabited. Come along for the ride as Kyle
discovers what it takes to become a Cavanaugh.

In closing, I thank you for reading, and with all my heart, I
wish you someone to love who loves you back.

As ever,

*Marie Ferrarella*

USA TODAY BESTSELLING AUTHOR

# MARIE FERRARELLA

## *Becoming a Cavanaugh*

Silhouette®

Romantic

SUSPENSE

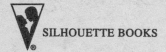

SILHOUETTE BOOKS

ISBN-13: 978-0-373-27645-5

Recycling programs
for this product may
not exist in your area.

BECOMING A CAVANAUGH

## Books by Marie Ferrarella

---

## MARIE FERRARELLA

This *USA TODAY* bestselling and RITA® Award-winning author has written more than one hundred and fifty books for Silhouette, some under the name Marie Nicole. Her romances are beloved by fans worldwide. Visit her Web site at www.marieferrarella.com.

To

Jaren Sterkel

Hope you like this one

# Chapter 1

Too much.

It was just too damn much to handle at the same time, Detective Kyle O'Brien thought as he walked out of his lieutenant's office.

His late mother used to be fond of saying that God never gave you more than you could handle. Obviously, this had to be the new, improved God heaping all this on him. Either that, or his mother wasn't really as close to the Man upstairs as she thought. All this was more than he could put up with at one time.

It had been hard enough dealing with his mother's recent death without finding out that she had lied to him, to his brother and to his sister for the last twenty-five years.

All of their lives.

Their father hadn't been a Marine who had died overseas for his country. Their biological father had actually been the late, malcontented Mike Cavanaugh, a police detective who had never married their mother because he already had a wife and family. From what Kyle had managed to gather, unlike his older brother Andrew and his younger brother Brian—both high-ranking officials on the Aurora police force—Mike Cavanaugh selfishly preferred the company of a bottle to that of anyone around him.

The revelation, made by his mother on her deathbed, had hit Kyle like the full swing of a sledgehammer right to his gut. What made it even worse was that they were the last words his mother uttered.

Angry at the immediate world and feeling deprived of his mother and the illusion of the father he'd *thought* he had and his very identity, Kyle had gone storming over to Andrew Cavanaugh's house to confront the former chief of police with this information.

At the time, Kyle had believed that everyone else in the vast Cavanaugh clan had known about Mike's indiscretions. As it turned out, Andrew Cavanaugh and the rest of the family were just as stunned by this latest twist as he and his siblings were.

None of the Cavanaughs were angered by this information, and he, Ethan and Greer suddenly found themselves welcomed into the family with open arms.

Well, almost everyone. It had taken Mike Cavanaugh's son, Patrick, a little while to come around.

But eventually—thanks to his wife and his sister—he had. The whole of the Cavanaughs had come around a great deal faster than he, Ethan and Greer had. Barely two months later, Greer was still a little in shock but coping. As for Ethan, he seemed to be acclimating to the reality of who his father was.

Funny, when you're part of triplets, you expect the other two-thirds to feel exactly the same way as you do. He supposed he couldn't fault them and in a way, he envied Ethan and Greer the peace that seemed to be coming into their lives.

But here he was, still trying to work through his hurt, his anger and his confusion, not to mention his grief. And if that wasn't enough on his plate, his partner up and quit the force.

Oh, he hadn't called it quitting. Eric Castle called what he was doing *retiring,* saying something about wanting to enjoy his life before his luck ran out. Whatever the hell he chose to call it, it felt like desertion.

Castle had been his first and only partner and he'd worked out a system with the older detective. One that served him pretty well. Now he was supposed to just skip off happily into some other partnership? With a Cheshire cat?

That was apparently what the lieutenant thought when he'd called him into his office.

Kyle sighed. He should have known something was up when he walked in and saw the woman sitting there in front of Lieutenant Barone's desk. A petite, pretty blonde, with lively blue eyes and a mouth that kept pulling into a smile as easily as she drew breath. Also as often. At first glance, he'd just assumed she was a friend of the lieutenant's. Maybe even his daughter, given the age spread.

The last thing she could be was his new partner. But then, he hadn't noticed the telltale bulge of her weapon.

His new partner.

The words stuck in his throat the first time he tried to repeat them. Finally, he managed to ask, his voice low, the words coming out almost on a growl, "You're replacing Castle?"

By the tolerant smile on the lieutenant's face, it was obvious that he'd expected resistance and had decided to be amused by it rather than annoyed. "Well, given that the man's on his way to Lake Arrowhead…" The indulgent smile widened as the lieutenant cocked his head, as if he was trying to read him. "Did you miss Castle's retirement party? Wasn't that you I saw giving the toast?" he prodded.

Kyle blew out an angry breath, but kept his expression blank. "Yeah, I know he's retired. I just thought you were going to let me go it alone for a while."

"I was," the lieutenant replied. "I believe my exact words were, 'You can go it alone until I can find you another partner.' And I did." He gestured toward the young woman in the other chair. "Detective Rosetti," he emphasized.

Kyle kept his unfathomable eyes on the lieutenant. "It's only been a week."

Barone inclined his head. "So it has. I didn't want you

to get too used to being on your own. You need someone to watch your back." There was no arguing with the lieutenant's tone. "Rosetti's a transfer from the Oakland PD. As luck would have it, she's from the homicide division, so there won't be a breaking-in period." He ended with a smile aimed at the young woman.

"As luck would have it," Kyle murmured under his breath.

Right now, he wasn't feeling particularly lucky. Just the opposite. He didn't have the time or the inclination to babysit a novice, no matter what Barone claimed. The woman couldn't possibly be a seasoned detective. Not with that face.

A glimmer of Barone's temper surfaced. He tolerated a little stubbornness, but only for so long. "Look, it's not as if we're some bed-and-breakfast township where arguments are resolved by going, *rock, paper, scissors*. People have hot tempers here and they kill each other. We need all the good men—and women," Barone amended, nodding his head at the new detective by way of a semi-apology for his near oversight, "we can get. Am I right?" he asked Kyle.

He knew there was no fighting this. "Yes, sir, you're always right."

Barone nodded his head. "Good of you to remember that. All right, I'll leave it up to you to show Detective Rosetti her desk and introduce her around to the others." Barone was already turning his attention to the next matter on his desk.

"Right." Kyle eyed his superior. "Is that all, sir?"

There was humor in the brown eyes when they looked up at Kyle. "For now," the lieutenant allowed.

Kyle turned on his heel and walked out. By the rustling noise behind him, he knew that his new albatross was shadowing his tracks.

"It's Jaren," he heard her call after him.

Kyle stopped, and turned around. The woman stopped an inch short of colliding into him. "What's Jaren?"

"My first name," she told him cheerfully. "You didn't ask."

"No, I didn't."

Because he didn't care. He'd been working with Castle for three months before he learned the man's first name. Things like that weren't necessary to do a good job. He wasn't looking for a relationship or a friendship, he was just looking to execute his job to the best of his abilities. Knowing her first name didn't figure into that.

Looking just a little at a loss as to how to read him, Jaren said, "So, now you know."

"Now I know," he echoed, his voice utterly emotionless.

Her eyes met his. He could swear he saw a bevy of questions forming and multiplying. It was like looking into a kaleidoscope as it rolled down a hill. "Can I know yours?"

Several retorts came to his lips and then slipped away. It wasn't her fault that he'd been saddled with her, he argued. Wasn't her fault that his mother had lied to him, and then chosen not to go to her grave with the secret that he and his siblings were bastards, fathered by a man who didn't care enough to form any sort of relationship with them, or their mother. Wasn't even her fault that his partner had left the force, leaving him exposed for just this sort of thing.

But damn, the perky little blonde was the only one here and he had no place else at the moment to discharge his temper.

"It's Kyle," he finally said. "Look—Rosetti is it?" Her eyes still holding his, she nodded. "You'd better know this up front. I've got my own way of getting things done."

Her smile was more amused than anything else. Why did that annoy him?

"I kind of figured that out. Don't worry, I won't get in your way, Kyle," she promised, her voice so cheerful it instantly grated on his nerves. "I'm just here to do my job, same as you."

He sincerely doubted that. Rosetti didn't suddenly have a *name* to live up to, didn't have to prove that she was every bit as good as the others who legitimately bore the name of Cavanaugh. He was no one's poor relation and the only way he could show his newfound *family* that he was just as good as they were was by being faster, better, smarter than all of them.

Hell of a tall order considering that the other Cavanaughs on the force—practically an army of them— were all top-notch cops, every last one of them. Still, he swore in his heart he was more than up to the challenge.

He and his brother and sister were up to the challenge, Kyle amended. Sometimes he tended to forget that he didn't need to feel as if he was the leader of the group. Just because he'd been born a full five minutes first didn't mean that he was the big brother. He'd always felt as if he was the protective one, the one who had to take care of everything for his siblings and his widowed mother.

Widowed. What a crock, he silently jeered, his heart hurting even as he did so.

*Why the hell didn't you trust us enough to tell us the truth when we were kids, Ma? Why build up a legend for a man who never even existed? Was it to make us feel better? Or did you make up those lies to make yourself feel better?*

He had no answer, only anger.

Kyle realized that his so-called new partner was looking at him as if she was waiting for an answer to something.

"What?" he snapped out impatiently.

They were out in the squad room and without thinking, he'd walked over to his own desk. Castle's had faced his. The surface was wiped clean. Hadn't been that clean since the first day he'd walked into this room.

"Is this my desk?" Jaren asked. There was no sign of impatience in her voice.

What was she, a robot? Just what he needed, someone who was always sunny. "That was Castle's desk," he answered.

"Your old partner."

It wasn't a guess. Jaren had done her homework. She always did. As bright and chipper as a cartoon character, she knew that people tended to underestimate her, and initially assumed that she probably had the IQ of a freshly laundered pink sock. Not wanting to surrender her natural personality and force herself to appear more somber than she was, she worked hard to negate that impression in other ways.

One of those ways was to be a walking encyclopedia on a great many subjects. The other was to be the best damn detective she could. This included being up on almost everything, including weapon proficiency. She mentioned none of this, preferring to surprise her detractors with displays when they were called for. It usually put them in their place after the first couple of times or so.

O'Brien, she decided, was going to take a bit of work.

"Yeah," Kyle answered grudgingly. "My old partner."

It wasn't that he felt lost without the older man, who'd been a decent mentor. It was just that Castle understood that he liked to keep his own counsel unless he had something important to say. Silence was a great part of their working relationship.

This one struck him as someone who only stopped talking if her head was held under water. And maybe not even then.

She nodded her head, curly, dark blond hair bobbing. "Then I guess that makes it mine."

"For now," he qualified. Despite what he'd said to the lieutenant, he was still very far from committed to this so-called partnership.

Her smile made him think of a mother indulging her child's fantasy. But only so far.

"I'm not going anywhere," she informed him pleasantly. "Unless, of course, they decide to move us. *En masse.*"

He grunted in response as he took his seat. Hitting a few keys, he appeared absorbed by what he saw on his monitor. His question took her by surprise, especially since she didn't think he asked questions, not of the people he worked with. She'd heard he was a pretty terrific detective, though, and she was hoping to learn something from him.

"Why'd you leave Oakland?"

"Personal reasons." When he merely nodded at her answer, Jaren asked, "Don't you want to know what they were?"

His eyes answered her before his words did. "Not particularly. Someone says something's personal, I figure they want to keep it that way."

She shook her head, allowing a small laugh to escape. It almost sounded lyrical. She would have a melodic laugh, he thought darkly. They'd hooked him up with a wood nymph.

"No, I was just labeling them. Personal as opposed to professional." Then, before he could cut her off, she filled him in—whether or not he wanted her to, she thought. "I left because my father died, and there was suddenly nothing left for me in Oakland. I have no family," she confided. "So, I sold my house and applied for a job down here."

*I've got too much family,* he thought. *Want some of mine?* Out loud he asked, "You're kind of young to be a detective, aren't you?"

She all but radiated pride as she answered. "Youngest to make the grade in Oakland," she confirmed. "The Chief of Ds said I was an eager beaver."

"Terrific."

Jaren waited for a moment. When her unwilling new partner said nothing further, she took the initiative. "So, what would you like me to do?"

"Stop talking, for one," Kyle answered without skipping a beat, or looking up from the folder he'd opened on his desk.

Rather than back away, she asked another question. "I take it you're the strong, silent type?"

He made a mental note to stop at the hardware store and buy a roll of duct tape. The clear kind so people wouldn't immediately notice that Rosetti's mouth was taped over.

"Something like that."

He heard her laugh softly to herself. "I've run into that before."

"I bet you have."

Jaren leaned over her empty new desk in order to get closer to him. "Don't worry, O'Brien, you'll find that working with me won't be such a bad thing."

Abandoning what he was trying to read, Kyle finally raised his head. He gave her a long, penetrating look. Had he met her off the job and a year ago, when he thought he knew who and what he was, and when the world was still recognizable to him, he might have even been attracted to her—once she learned not to talk so much. But now, well, now he had a feeling he would count himself lucky if he didn't strangle her by the end of the day.

"We'll see," he said, his voice showing no glimmer of hope in that direction.

Suddenly, his new partner was on her feet again like a Pop-Tart escaping a toaster. "I'm going for coffee," she told him. "Can I get you any?"

"No, thanks." She took five steps before she stopped and turned around again. He had a feeling that she would. "What?"

"Where is the coffee machine?" she asked, her demeanor so sunny it just blackened his mood.

Kyle sighed and began to point in the general direction where the machines were located, then remembered that they had been moved last week. If he were still a churchgoer, he would have thought of this woman as penance.

Reluctantly, he pushed back his chair and rose to his feet. "C'mon, I'll show you."

He didn't think it was humanly possible for her to brighten, but she did. "Thank you, that's very nice of you."

"No, it's not," he denied, walking out of the squad room and into the hallway. "For the record, it's called self-preservation. If you're drinking, you won't be talking."

His sarcastic remark earned him yet another grin. "I'll try to keep it down," she promised.

"If only," Kyle murmured to himself under his breath. He had a feeling she heard him because she slanted an amused look in his direction.

The vending machines' new location wasn't that far

away from the elevators. They were almost there when he heard a woman call out his name. They both turned around, Kyle almost unwillingly, and Jaren with the bright enthusiasm of a newcomer who was eager to absorb her surroundings as quickly as she could.

He found himself facing Riley McIntyre, newly attached to the Cavanaugh clan herself, as were her two brothers, Zack and Frank, and her older sister, Taylor.

At this rate, the Cavanaughs were going to be able to populate their own small city, he thought cynically.

He saw her giving the woman beside him a quick, scrutinizing look. This almost constant sharing of his life was new to him and he didn't much like it. "Heard you got a new partner, Kyle. This her?"

She obviously waited for an introduction, but was never one to stand on ceremony. "Hi, I'm Jaren Rosetti," Jaren said, extending her hand to the woman.

Riley wrapped her fingers around Jaren's hand. "I'm Riley McIntyre, Kyle's stepcousin." Riley's eyes danced as she made the introduction.

Okay, that was a new one, Jaren thought. She looked from the blonde to Kyle. If any explanation was coming, Riley would do the honors. Getting words out of Kyle O'Brien was like pulling teeth. Very strong teeth.

"Stepcousin?" Jaren repeated.

Riley nodded. "My mother recently married Brian Cavanaugh. He's the chief of detectives here. And Kyle's his nephew. That makes me his stepcousin. There're four of us on the force—stepcousins," Riley qualified, flashing a grin at the younger woman. "Don't worry, it gets easier as time goes on," she said.

"Not hardly," Kyle muttered to himself. Looking for a way to garner a few seconds of peace and quiet, he decided to do what he ordinarily never did—ask for a favor. "Riley, can you show her where the coffee machine is?"

Riley shrugged. "No problem. I was on my way there myself."

And the next minute, Jaren found herself being taken under the wing of a Cavanaugh by marriage. Any misgivings she might have entertained about transferring to Aurora's police department quickly faded away in the face of Riley's sunny disposition and easy manner.

She was going to like it here, Jaren decided.

# Chapter 2

"I brought you some coffee."

She was back, Kyle thought. So much for peace and quiet.

He glanced up from the report he was finishing. He hated the paperwork that went along with the job, and it was hard enough tackling it when he was in a good frame of mind. This was going to take him all day.

His new partner, Mary Sunshine, stood there, holding in each hand a container of what passed for coffee at the precinct.

"I don't remember asking you to," he said, making no attempt to take either container from her.

"You didn't," she answered, keeping a smile on her face. "I just thought you might like to have a cup. Newest studies say that three cups of coffee a day help keep your memory sharp."

Part of him knew he was being unreasonable and ornery, but he just didn't feel friendly at the moment. And for her own good, Rosetti had better understand his moodiness early on.

"And just why would you think that you have to appoint yourself the guardian of my memory?" he asked.

Jaren placed the container she'd brought back for him on his desk, then sat down at hers. She studied him for a moment.

"You know, I'd say that you got up on the wrong side of the bed today, but I've got a feeling that today, there wouldn't have been a right side." She paused to take a sip of her coffee, then asked, "Or is that just a given?"

Kyle didn't bother giving her an answer. Instead, he just looked back at the paperwork on his desk.

She sighed, but refused to give up. "Look, I'm trying to make nice here."

He raised his eyes, meeting hers for a fleeting second. "Don't."

There was no such thing as *don't* in her language. Jaren tried again, relying on logic, something she felt probably appealed to him. "Until one of us transfers or dies or they rearrange the room, we're going to be stuck facing each other like this five days a week. Don't you think it would make things a little easier on both of us if you stopped acting as if I'm the devil incarnate?"

"Nope."

She sighed and shook her head. "I think you should know I don't give up easy."

She wished he didn't look so damn sexy as he raised his eyes again and said, "You do what you have to do, and I'll do what I have to do."

She had no idea if she was being warned, put on notice or dismissed. But she wasn't about to put up with any of that.

Before she could think of something to say in return, she saw the lieutenant walking toward them. Barone held a slip of paper with writing on it in his hand.

"Dispatch called to say a hysterical receptionist just got in to the office to find the doctor she worked for— a Richard Barrett—dead." The lieutenant held out the slip of paper that contained pertinent information, including the address. "You two are up."

Mentally, Kyle winced. He wasn't ready to work a case with Little Miss Perky, but there was apparently nothing he could do about it. Resigned, Kyle pushed himself away from his desk. But by the time he got to his feet, Jaren had taken the slip of paper from Barone.

"We're on it," she assured Barone as she slid her arms through the sleeves of her jacket.

Frowning, Kyle confiscated the slip of paper from her and glanced at the address. He spared the lieutenant a look as he shoved the paper into his pocket. "Pricey part of town."

"Rich people get killed, too," Barone replied. "The details are a little freaky, so get back to me on this as soon as possible."

"What do you mean by freaky?" Jaren asked before Kyle could voice the same question.

The woman had a mouth set in fast-forward, he thought darkly.

"You'll see," was all Barone promised.

*"Freaky* doesn't begin to cover this one," Kyle commented under his breath as he looked down at the slain doctor. Parts of the expensive Persian rug he lay on was discolored. Blood oozed from the man's chest.

Dr. Richard Barrett was a respected, well-known neurosurgeon whose skill was only equaled by his ego. Said to be almost a miracle worker, his services were sought from all over the country. Consequently, he had an incredibly long waiting list.

According to what Barrett's receptionist told them in whispered confidence, as if the dead surgeon could still somehow hear her, he'd had the bedside manner of Attila the Hun.

"Care to be more specific about that?" Kyle prodded the nervous young woman.

"He always made you feel as if you were beneath him," Carole Jenkins told them. She averted her eyes from the slain figure on the floor. The sight of him had made her turn a very unbecoming shade of green. "To be honest, I think Dr. Barrett even felt he was above God."

Jaren glanced down at the man's face, frozen in horror. That kind of an attitude would have won the neurosurgeon no friends.

"So, you're saying that Dr. Barrett had a lot of enemies?" Jaren asked.

The receptionist backpedaled a little, as if she didn't want to speak ill of the dead. "He had a lot of grateful patients," she assured them hastily, and then relented, "but yes, he did have a lot of people who didn't like him. I don't know if you'd call them enemies, but he had a tendency to rub everyone the wrong way. But I never thought…" Her voice trailed off as she glanced at the body on the floor and then shivered.

Kyle squatted down beside the body, his attention focused on the large wooden stake protruding from the man's chest.

"Death by wooden stake. Don't think I've ever come across that before," he said more to himself than to his partner. "This does seem to be a little extreme."

"I'll—I'll be in the next room if you need me," Carole stammered, already backing away from them—and the corpse. "I—I just can't—"

Giving her a comforting smile, Jaren took the woman's arm and escorted her out of the doctor's study.

"You just sit down at your desk and we'll get back to you if we have any more questions," she said kindly. Turning around, she appraised the slain surgeon. The stake had been driven into the middle of his chest. Deeply. "Think it's a statement?"

Kyle glanced at her over his shoulder. "That someone hated him?"

She was going for something a bit more colorful. "That someone thought of him as a vampire."

Kyle stared at her as if she'd lost her mind. "Come again?"

"Are you baiting me?" she asked. A frown was the only answer she received. Humoring the man, she went into detail. "Everyone knows that the only way to kill a vampire is to drive a stake through his heart."

It didn't make any sense to him. They weren't living in the Middle Ages, they were living in an enlightened society. "So, someone was calling Barrett a vampire?"

"Blood sucker, most likely. Maybe they were protesting his fee. Or a surgery that went wrong," she suddenly guessed. In her opinion, those could have all been viable reasons for murder, given the right person.

Kyle wasn't ready to grant that she'd had an interesting theory just yet. "Don't you think that's a little off the wall?" he scoffed.

"To you and me, yes," she agreed. "But maybe not to the killer." And it was the killer's mind they were attempting to assess.

Jaren had pulled on a pair of rubber gloves the minute they'd gotten off the elevator on the third floor. As Kyle examined the doctor more closely, she went through the surgeon's things on his desk and shelves, looking for a lead.

When she came to a black-bound, hardcover book, she paused. There it was, in plain sight on the shelf behind his desk.

"Well, how about that."

The bemused note in her voice caught his attention.

Though he wanted to pretend he hadn't heard her, something about the woman was hard to ignore.

"What?"

Jaren turned from the shelves, holding a thick volume in her hands. "The good doctor's reading material might have given our killer the idea."

Damn but he missed his old partner's monotone, straightforward voice. When Castle talked, it wasn't in circles. "What the hell are you talking about?"

Jaren held up the book she'd found.

*"The Vampire Diaries,"* Kyle read and then scoffed. "Who reads trash like that?"

His reaction to the book didn't surprise her. "Apparently, enough people to put this on the *New York Times* bestseller list for several weeks."

Few things caught him off guard, but she'd scored a point. "You're kidding me."

"I don't think it's possible to kid you," she added when he eyed her curiously. "But to answer your question, no, I'm not kidding. *The Vampire Diaries* has been on the list for close to five weeks now." She flipped some of the pages. "Not a bad story, as far as things like that go."

Kyle stared at her as if she'd just announced that she was an extra terrestrial, sent down to conquer Earth. "You read it?"

If he was trying to embarrass her, he was going to have to do a lot better than that, Jaren thought wickedly. "Yes, I did. I wanted to see what the fuss was about. I like leaving myself open to new experiences—like

getting along with a partner who acts as if he's con-
stantly got a bur under his saddle."

Kyle didn't appear to hear her, or, if he did, he was
ignoring her comment and focusing on what she'd said
before that. He circled the dead man, taking the body
in at all angles.

"Vampires, huh?"

Jaren shrugged. "Some women find fantasizing about
vampires romantic."

He laughed shortly, letting her know what he thought
of that. "Some women marry prisoners who have no
chance of getting out."

"Takes all kinds," she agreed. "Besides," Jaren
quipped, "the woman who marries a lifer always knows
where he is at night." He looked at her. "And before you
ask, yes, I'm kidding."

"You guys mind taking this to the next room?" asked
a tall, gangly man wearing what looked like paper
scrubs over his regular clothing. He was one of three
crime-scene investigators who had been sent to go over
the doctor's office, preserving it just as it had been when
the receptionist found Barrett.

"No problem. We need to ask Carole for a list of the
doctor's most recent patients," Jaren told the investigator agreeably. She leaned over and extended her hand.
"I'm Jaren Rosetti, by the way."

"Hank Elder," the investigator responded, shaking
her hand.

"Carole?" Kyle asked as they exited the doctor's study.

"The receptionist," she told him.

He stopped short of the woman's desk. "I don't recall her giving us her name."

"That's because she didn't," Jaren told him. "She's wearing a name tag."

He'd been too interested in the weapon used to kill the surgeon to notice all that much about the woman who had called the murder in.

"I tend not to look at a woman's chest area," he said. "Avoids problems."

"It's okay, that's what you've got me for."

Kyle suppressed another sigh. "Knew there was a reason."

Carole obliged them with an extensive list of the names of the neurosurgeon's patients in the last six months.

"When did this man sleep?" Jaren wondered out loud as she scanned the names.

"I don't think he did," Carole confided. "According to what I heard, the doctor was burning the candle at both ends."

Kyle took the list from Jaren and folded it, putting it into his pocket. "Was he married?"

The receptionist pushed her glasses up on her nose before she shook her head. "Divorced. Twice."

Kyle nodded as if he'd expected to hear something like that. "We'll need his ex-wives' addresses, as well," he told the receptionist.

Carole caught her lower lip between her teeth. She was obviously thinking.

"I'd have to get in touch with one of his colleagues at the hospital to get those for you. Dr. Barrett doesn't have that kind of information accessible on his computer." Her expression was apologetic. "He is—was—extremely private that way."

Jaren looked toward the study. The three crime-scene investigators had left the door open. They were combing the area but all she could see was the body on the rug.

"Could be a crime of passion," she speculated. She turned back to Carole. "You wouldn't know if Barrett had any current girlfriends, would you?"

Carole's short brown hair swung from side to side as she shook her head. "Like I said, Dr. Barrett was very private."

"That's okay, we'll ask around. And if you can think of anything else—" Jaren reached into her pocket to give the young woman her card, then stopped. She flashed an apologetic smile. "I'm afraid I don't have any cards printed up with my cell number on them yet." She turned toward her partner. "O'Brien?"

"Yeah, I got one." Reaching into his pocket, he took out a card and handed it to the receptionist. Despite the gruesome scene in the other room, Carole smiled up at him. For a moment, she seemed to forget about the circumstances that had brought them together.

"Thank you," she murmured.

"Guess I'm due for a hearing test," Kyle commented as they walked out of the office several minutes later.

"Excuse me?" Jaren asked.

"Well, I'm obviously not hearing as well as I should

be." Reaching the elevator bank, he pressed the down button. "Because if I were, I would have heard Barone say that you were primary on this."

The elevator arrived. She stepped inside and turned toward the front. They were the only two people in the car. "Sorry. I tend to be a little enthusiastic."

He laughed as the doors closed again. "Is that what you call it?"

She knew she was going to hate herself for this. "What would you call it?"

"Being a pain in the butt."

The best way to deal with things was through humor. She reverted to it now. "Potato, po-ta-to," she replied with a quick shrug of her shoulders. She saw him taking the list that Carole had given them out of his pocket. She nodded at it. "So, how do you want to do this?"

What he wanted to say was *alone,* but he knew that wasn't going to get him anywhere. She apparently had the sticking power of super glue. Still, he decided to give it one try. "We could divide the list between us."

"I'm still new here," she reminded him. "I would have thought that, since you're primary on this," she deliberately emphasized, "you'd want to question these people together—to make sure I don't mess up."

He wasn't in the mood for sarcasm. "Rosetti, I don't want to do anything together," he told her, "but it looks like I have no choice."

The elevator came to a stop and they got out on the ground floor. She followed him out of the building.

"Tell me, is it just me who sets you off, or is it having a partner in general?"

"Yes."

The single word hung in the air. Jaren took a breath. This had the makings of one hell of a long day. "Okay," she declared, as if she knew where she stood.

And she did. Barefoot in hell. But she'd survived worse and she was going to survive this. She made herself a solemn vow that she would.

Their next stop was the hospital where Richard Barrett performed his mini miracles—skillfully reattaching nerve endings against defying odds. Everyone they spoke to on the floor attested to the fact that the surgeon had no equal. On a scale of one to ten, he was a twelve.

But when it came to being human, that number dropped to a two.

The woman in the administration office was able to provide them with the names and addresses of both the former Mrs. Barretts.

Armed with both the list of patients and the addresses of his ex-wives, Kyle made the decision to interview the latter first. Sixty percent of the time, whenever a homicide victim was married or estranged, the search for the killer had to go no further than that person's spouse or former lover.

As it turned out, spouse number one was immediately dismissed. According to the doorman at the apartment building where she lived, Wanda Barrett had become Wanda Davenport a little over a week ago and was currently in Spain on her honeymoon with her brand-new husband. The doorman said he'd never seen the woman look so happy. For the time being, they believed him.

Spouse number two wasn't out of the country, she was in her apartment. Once Kyle identified himself and his partner and told the woman the reason they were there, Alison Barrett, a slightly overweight brunette with scarlet nails and a mouth that formed a wide frown, became livid.

"That bastard!" she shrieked. With a swing of her hand, she knocked over a statue of Cupid that had been perched on a pedestal. It hit the marble floor, shattering. In her fury, she appeared not to notice. "He finally found a way to get around paying me alimony."

Jaren glanced at Kyle to see his reaction to this display of unbridled temper. "With all due respect, Mrs. Barrett," she said, "I don't think that death by wooden stake would have been his first choice to avoid making payments to you."

"You didn't know Richard," she fumed, pacing. "Life with him was hell and I thought that now, at long last, I'd be compensated for it." Her eyes flashed with unsuppressed fury. "But he found a way to wiggle out of it."

"Your grief is touching," Kyle commented.

Her eyes blazed. "You want grief, Detective? Grief was being married to him and being treated as if I was some sub-intelligent species. He thought he was God and should have been worshipped accordingly."

"If you felt that way about him, why did you marry him in the first place?" Jaren wanted to know.

Alison sighed, frustrated. "Because Richard could be very charming when he wanted. The problem was, once we were married, he didn't want to be. He was out all day, out all night. Like some damn werewolf."

Jaren's eyes met Kyle's. The exchange was not missed by the victim's ex-wife. She quickly backpedaled.

"Not that I thought he was one," she assured them. "Or a vampire," she added for good measure. "What he was—and everyone who knew him knew this—was a self-centered bastard."

That made the opinion unanimous, Kyle thought. He had a feeling that they were going to have their hands full with suspects.

"Just for the record, Mrs. Barrett, where were you this afternoon?"

"Where I am every afternoon," she replied haughtily. "Shopping. It's one of my few pleasures."

"Anyone see you shopping?"

She blew out an angry breath, as if this was a huge inconvenience. "I went with friends. I have receipts," she volunteered. "I didn't want to see him dead, Detective. I wanted to have him pay through the nose."

"Thank you for your time," Kyle told the woman once she produced the time-stamped sales receipts to back her up. "We'll see ourselves out."

As they left the opulent apartment, they could hear Alison Barrett heaping curses on her ex-husband's dead head.

"Woman makes a good case for the single life," Kyle commented more to himself than to Jaren as they closed the door behind them.

So do you, Jaren thought, but she decided to keep her observation to herself.

## Chapter 3

Kyle glanced at his watch after he buckled his seat belt. He'd more or less promised to be somewhere. His exact words, when he'd received the invitation, were, "We'll see." The look on Andrew Cavanaugh's face had told him that he was going to wind up coming. He supposed it wouldn't do any harm to give this family thing a try.

"It's after five," Kyle announced, addressing his words more to the windshield than to the woman next to him. "Why don't we call it a day and get a fresh start in the morning?"

The suggestion surprised her. She would have thought that O'Brien would have wanted to push both of them to the point of exhaustion—probably just to see what she was made of.

She was relieved to find out that she was wrong. "Sounds good to me."

Like all first days on the job, this one had felt endless, going on much longer than eight hours. It would feel good to go home and unwind, she thought, even though *home* right now was an apartment filled with boxes waiting to be unpacked. Towers of boxes that made maneuvering around the premises a challenge.

But at least she'd get the chance to chill out for a few hours.

Despite a minor traffic snarl due to a two-car collision on the next block, they got back to the precinct in a fairly short amount of time. Getting out on her side, Jaren paused. The ride back had consisted of her talking in between the silences. O'Brien's contributions to the conversation had been limited to occasional grunts, and even those she had to prod out of him.

Still, Jaren thought it might be worth a try to ask. The worst that could happen would be another grunt. "You know anywhere around here where I could get a decent meal? I'd prefer take-out, but if I have to sit at a restaurant, that's okay, too."

Kyle peered at her over the top of the car for a long moment, debating. And then, because he knew he hadn't been a joy to work with and the days that were ahead probably wouldn't be any better, he made an impulsive decision, something he didn't ordinarily do.

"Yeah," he finally said, "I do."

Maybe he got more human at the end of the day, she thought. "Really?"

Kyle frowned. "You sound surprised."

"Well, I guess I am," she confessed. What surprised her even more was that he seemed to actually be willing to tell her about the place. She'd half expected him to snap out a *no*.

"If you didn't think I knew of a place, why did you ask?"

One slim shoulder rose and fell in a gesture that he found, if he were being honest, oddly appealing. Kyle forced himself to focus on her face instead.

"There was always an outside chance," Jaren replied. "And to be honest, after dragging almost every word out of you today, what I'm really surprised about is that you're willing to share the information."

He didn't make it an outright invitation. Instead, what he said was, "Best meals in town are at Andrew Cavanaugh's house."

"Andrew Cavanaugh," Jaren repeated, processing the name. It seemed to her that every third law enforcement officer at the precinct was named Cavanaugh. It took her a second to place this one. "Isn't that the name of the old chief of police?"

To her delight, she heard Kyle laugh. It was a short, quick sound, but it was a laugh nonetheless. "Don't let him catch you calling him old."

"I didn't mean old as in old," she explained quickly. "I meant old as in former. Anyway, he's a person, I'm looking for a restaurant."

He knew Andrew's philosophy. The more, the merrier. He'd thought it was a myth—before he ever had a blood connection to the man—that Cavanaugh had what amounted to a bottomless refrigerator. The myth was that Andrew never ran out of food no matter how many people showed up at his table. Now that he'd been witness to it several times, Kyle knew this was actually a fact, as incredible as it seemed.

Having Rosetti come along with him would provide no hardship for Cavanaugh. The opposite would probably be true. "I thought maybe you were looking for a memorable meal."

At this point, she'd settle for something that didn't repeat endlessly on her throughout the night. "Well, yes, but—"

His voice had a disinterested ring to it as he told her, "Doesn't get any better than what Andrew Cavanaugh can whip up. Even his throwaways are better than most restaurants' featured specials of the day."

He really did think she was pushy, didn't he? "That might be, but even if I did know where the man lived, I couldn't just go barging in and show up for dinner." He surprised her by laughing in response. She looked at him in confusion. Was he pulling her leg? "Did I say something funny?"

"From what I've gathered—and I've only interacted with the man a handful of times—that's exactly what you can do."

"I don't understand."

"The chief likes to cook and he really seems to like

having his family around him. In his opinion, the best way he can get them to keep coming back is to keep feeding them."

O'Brien had missed one very important point, she thought. "I'm not family."

The glimmer of a smile intrigued her. Or was that a sneer? With him it was hard to tell.

"You are if you're a cop," he told her.

He had no idea why he was extending the invitation or saying any of this to her. The entire day, all he could think about was getting into his car and going home—to silence. At the very most, maybe he'd call Ethan or Greer to see how their day went. He'd already made up his mind that he wasn't going to show up at Andrew's tonight for the party.

But for some reason he couldn't quite fathom, he'd changed his mind. He knew that the former chief of police felt personally guilty for the way Kyle and his siblings had been physically and emotionally abandoned by the man responsible for bringing them into the world in the first place.

Ordinarily, someone else's guilt was none of Kyle's concern, but Cavanaugh had tried to do right by them. He supposed that not showing up tonight would be an insult. It'd be tantamount to throwing the man's hospitality in his face.

That he felt a certain obligation to go was understandable. The real mystery was why he was asking Rosetti to come with him.

Maybe it was as simple as just feeling sorry for her. And then again, maybe not.

"I was thinking of dropping over there tonight. He's having some kind of gathering," Kyle explained vaguely. "If you wanted to tag along…" He left the rest unsaid.

There was silence for exactly two seconds.

"Sure. Yes. That would be very nice." Eagerness increased with every word she uttered. And then she shook her head. "You know, O'Brien, you're a damn hard man to figure out."

Kyle had a perfect solution for that. "Then don't try."

"Now that sounds more like you," Jaren responded, grinning. "Look, I just have to get my car. I'll follow you over to the house."

He took out his worn notebook, vaguely realizing that there were only three empty sheets left. Kyle turned to a fresh one and wrote something down, then tore it out and held it out to her.

"Here's the chief's address. In case you get lost," he added when she raised a quizzical brow.

There was no chance of that, he thought as he drove to the chief's house. Jaren Rosetti followed closer than a heartbeat, leaving hardly enough room between his car and hers for a thin mint.

When he pulled up to the curb, she was right there behind him, matching movement for movement. "You know," he said as he got out of his car, "if there'd been an eager cop around, you could have gotten a ticket for tailgating."

"Lucky there was no eager cop around," she coun- tered, amused. They both knew that uniforms didn't issue tickets to detectives unless gross misconduct was involved. Jaren examined the house number they'd parked in front of and turned to him. "This isn't the address you gave me."

"That's because there's no space left to park in front of the chief's house." He nodded toward the middle of the street. "It's one of their birthdays and he's throwing a party. Everyone was supposed to come."

That stopped her dead. "Birthday?" Jaren echoed. She suddenly felt awkward, not to mention empty- handed. "But I don't have anything to give."

"Why should you? You don't even know Callie." Callie was the chief's oldest daughter, married to the judge whose kidnapped daughter she'd helped rescue.

He had a point, but he was missing the main one. "But if I don't even know her, why am I—?"

"You hungry or not?" he demanded.

"Hungry," she confirmed. Hungrier for company than she was for anything that could be served on a plate, she added silently. While she was comfortable enough in her own skin, she had to admit that she did like the sound of people's voices and she *really* enjoyed interacting with them.

"Then stop arguing and come on," he ordered.

Jaren hurried to catch up as he walked quickly down the block.

He was right. The entire way from where they parked to the front of Andrew's house was jammed with cars, all going nose to tailpipe. She didn't envy the owners when they attempted to free their rides in order to go home.

Music greeted them before they ever reached the house, as did the sound of laughter. Andrew Cavanaugh's house seemed to exude warmth.

Walking up to the front door, Kyle didn't bother ringing the bell. Instead, he knocked on the door. Hard.

When there was no response, he tried the doorknob and found it wasn't locked.

"He leaves his door unlocked?" she asked, stunned. The neighborhood where she'd lived with her father had slowly gone downhill. By the time she'd sold the place, the front door had been outfitted with double locks coupled with a chain.

Kyle glanced at her over his shoulder just as he opened the door. "If you were a thief, would you walk into this?"

*This* was practically a wall of people, mostly detectives with their spouses and children. There was also a smattering of uniformed officers who'd come straight from work.

"Not unless I had a death wish," she agreed. It looked as if half the precinct had gathered here. There wasn't a solemn face in the lot.

This was it, Jaren realized. This was exactly what she'd longed for all of her life. Enough family stuffed into a house to make the very walls groan and bow. As far back as she could remember, there'd only been her parents and her. And, from the time she turned twelve—when her mother had decided that she'd just had enough and walked out, never to be heard from again—there'd been only her and her father.

Officer Joseph Rosetti had been a handsome man, quick to smile, quick to tell a joke and quick to raise a glass in a toast—even if he was the only one in the room. Most of her childhood had been spent either taking care of her father, or searching the local bars for his whereabouts in order to bring him home. Despite his shortcomings, Jaren loved him dearly and she knew that, in his own way, her father had loved her, too.

Just not enough to conquer the grip that alcohol had on him.

More than once when she was growing up, she'd found herself wishing that there was someone she could turn to—an aunt, an uncle, a sibling or grandparent—just someone with a few good words to cheer her on and buoy her up. But the only family she had was a man who seemed intent on pickling his liver one bottle at a time.

Eventually, he had. Liver failure claimed him, taking him, in her opinion, years before his time.

Lost in thought and wishful thinking as she scanned the large group of people, she suddenly felt a large hand on her shoulder. Turning, she saw a tall, smiling man with the kindest blue eyes she'd ever seen. He'd placed himself between her and her new partner.

Instinctively, she knew this had to be Andrew Cavanaugh.

"You came!" he exclaimed, his booming voice echoing with both pleasure and surprise. He turned approving eyes toward the young woman with his brother's son. "And you brought someone with you."

Kyle nodded. "This is my new partner, Andrew. She's

new to Aurora and she asked me if I knew anyplace that served really good food."

"And you brought her to me," Andrew concluded, pleased. "Well, young lady, I hope you don't come away disappointed. By the way, Kyle forgot to introduce us. I'm Andrew Cavanaugh."

"Yes, I know," Jaren said, shaking his hand. His grip was firm and warm. She noted that he didn't insult her by weakening his grip in deference to her softer gender. She liked that. Nothing worse than a limp-wristed handshake. "My name is Jaren. Jaren Rosetti."

"Rosetti," Andrew repeated. His eyebrows drew together as he thought for a moment. "I used to know a Joe Rosetti. He was on the Oakland police force. Had an occasion to work with him early on. Great guy. Any relation?"

A spark of pride ignited. Until the end came when he had to be hospitalized, her father had somehow managed to be a functioning alcoholic, never drinking on the job, just continually from the moment he was off duty. He'd fooled a lot of people, she remembered.

"He was my father."

"Was?" The concern in Andrew's eyes was genuine. She liked him immediately.

Jaren nodded. "He died a couple of months ago." It was still hard for her to say that. Harder still to imagine a world without Joe Rosetti.

"Well, I'm sorry to hear that, Jaren. Your father was a good cop." Somewhere in the distance, a timer went off, but Andrew continued talking to the young woman his nephew had brought into his house. "He must have been proud to see you follow in his footsteps."

By the time she'd made it to the rank of detective, her father had retired from the force and been too wound up in his daily ritual of emptying wine bottles with Black Russian chasers to take much notice of anything.

Jaren knew that her smile was just a wee bit tight as she said, "I'd like to think so." Was it her imagination, or had the chief's eyes softened just a shade, as if he understood what wasn't being said?

Andrew turned toward his nephew. "Why don't you introduce Jaren around, Kyle? By the way, in case you're wondering, your brother and sister are already here. You were the last holdout," Andrew said with a soft laugh, as if he'd known all along that it would just be a matter of time before he was won over by the family. He clapped Kyle on the shoulder and said warmly, "Glad to see that you decided to make it. Wouldn't have been the same without you."

Kyle looked back into the house. The living room, the family room and parts beyond, including the backyard, were teeming with people.

"And how would you have noticed?" he asked dryly.

"Trust me," Andrew assured him, "I would have noticed." The timer sounded a second time. Andrew checked his watch. "If you'll excuse me, I've got to see to the main course."

"He really does cook, then?" Jaren asked.

Kyle laughed. "You don't know the half of it."

She had never really mastered the kitchen. The best

she could do was work with things that came in boxes and had the word *helper* in the title. Cooking for its own sake was a foreign concept to her. She'd been too busy juggling school, jobs—part-time and full—and caring for her delinquent father to spend any real time in the kitchen beyond cleaning up.

"He seems like a very nice man," she observed as she watched the former chief retreat into his state-of-the-art kitchen.

"Yeah." No matter how he felt—or didn't feel—about becoming part of this close-knit clan, there was no denying the fact that Andrew Cavanaugh had done his damnedest to make the transition easy on all three of them. But he still wasn't completely convinced that he wanted in.

He became aware that his new partner was studying him. When he glanced over at her, she asked, "And you're actually related to him?"

He could see how she might doubt that, given their natures. "Yeah."

"How?" The single word had launched itself out of her mouth before she could think to stop it.

He blew out a breath. "Do you ever stop asking questions?"

"Sure. Once I get the answers."

Just because—in a moment of weakness he was beginning to regret—he'd felt sorry for her and brought her to this gathering, didn't mean that he was going to bare his soul to her.

"If you get all the answers," he told her, "then there's nothing to look forward to."

"Sure, there is," she contradicted. "More questions—and answers."

He wasn't about to be cornered into a game of truth or dare with this woman. "Don't make me regret bringing you here."

Jaren knew when to back off. "I'll do my best," she promised.

They stood in the doorway of the living room for perhaps ten seconds before they were approached by another one of the Cavanaughs. This time, it was Patience, the only Cavanaugh besides Janelle who wasn't a law-enforcement agent. Patience's vocation lay with curing animals. Her involvement with the police department, other than through her sibling, cousins and uncles, was by being the official vet for the K-9 unit. Which was how she'd met her husband.

She was also Mike's daughter and thus Kyle's half sister, a connection she more than readily embraced. As she came toward them now, there was the same mixture of pleasure and surprise evident in her face that her uncle had displayed.

She brushed her lips against Kyle's cheek, catching him off guard. "I didn't think you were going to make it," she confessed. Her eyes darted to Jaren's face, then back to her newly discovered half brother. "And you brought a date?" It was more of a question than an assertion.

"I brought my partner," Kyle corrected. "She was hungry and it's a known fact that Andrew's the best cook in town, so I just thought—"

Why was he even explaining himself? Kyle wondered. Maybe he shouldn't have shown up at all. More than that, a part of him regretted pushing for recognition as Mike Cavanaugh's son. He wasn't even completely certain why he'd pushed the way he had. What had he hoped to accomplish? It wasn't as if the man was still around to acknowledge the connection.

When he'd undertaken this little mission, he'd been prepared for fierce opposition. Just the opposite had occurred. He'd had dealings with the Cavanaughs before. Anyone who was on the force had had dealings with a member of the clan at one time or another. He'd always thought that they were a decent bunch of people. But even so, he'd expected them to be hostile to the idea that he and his siblings cast a shadow on Mike Cavanaugh's name by turning up and claiming to be his offspring.

Nothing could have been further from the truth. He still didn't quite understand why.

Patience hooked her arm through Jaren's. "So, his new partner, huh? This should be interesting," she prophesized. "By the way, I'm Patience, Kyle's half sister. We shared a father," she said matter-of-factly. "Let me take you around and introduce you, Jaren."

Jaren felt her mouth curving, reflecting the smile she felt inside. "Works for me."

Her smile didn't even fade as she heard Kyle instruct Patience, "Take your time. There's no hurry."

"He takes getting used to," Patience confided with a comforting smile. "But in the long run, we figure he's worth it."

"I've kind of figured that out myself," Jaren told her.

Patience looked at her for a long moment, her smile warm and welcoming. "My money's on you, Jaren."

"Nice to know," Jaren replied, the sentiment warming her heart.

# Chapter 4

"C'mon, Callie, tell us. How old are you?" Riley McIntyre teased as they all gathered around the birthday celebrant and the huge, three-tiered cake Andrew had baked, the last strains of an off-key rendition of "Happy Birthday" fading away. "You've got to be older than one."

One large white candle, a pink rose winding around its thick base, was all that stood atop the third tier. Callie had made her wish and blown it out to the sound of cheers, applause and laughter.

"Older than you," Callie responded with a toss of her head. Her eyes shone as she added, "That's all you need to know."

"My wife is ageless," Brent Montgomery informed Riley and anyone else who cared to make inquiries about Callie's chronological age. "Like fine wine, she just gets better with time."

Slipping her arm around Brent's waist, Callie inclined her head, resting it against his shoulder as she gave him a quick squeeze. "Knew there was a reason why I married this man."

"Yeah, 'cause he was the only one who wasn't fast enough to run for the hills," Clay, her younger brother and Teri's twin, chimed in. It earned him a swat to the back of his head from his wife, Ilene.

"I suggest we begin cutting the cake before someone gets tempted to start throwing it instead," Andrew told the gathering. He placed one of his prized knives in Callie's hand, moving the plates closer to her.

"You heard the man," Callie said to the rest of her family and friends. She made the first cut. "Line up if you don't want to be left out."

No one had to be told twice. Riley was first in line, but rather than take a plate and walk away, she began to pass out the slices as Callie cut them and placed them on the plates.

"Are they always like this?" Jaren asked. She was standing off to the side with Kyle, waiting for the crowd to thin down a little.

Kyle shook his head. "I wouldn't know. I'm new to this."

She slanted a knowing look in his direction. "That would explain it."

"Explain what?"

"Why you didn't sing 'Happy Birthday' when everyone else did." She'd been standing right next to him and had wondered why he hadn't joined in with the rest.

"I sang," he protested tersely.

"No, you moved your lips," she corrected. "But no sound came out of your mouth." She grinned at Kyle. "So, what we had was video, but no audio."

He was one of those people who couldn't carry a tune in a bucket and he knew it. He didn't particularly like calling attention to the fact.

"Maybe that was because I figured you'd take care of the audio all by yourself," he retorted.

She was a guest here and since he was the one who'd brought her, she wasn't about to get embroiled in an argument, no matter how innocuous it was. So she nodded. "Glad to pitch in."

Riley handed him a plate. He, in turn, passed the slice of vanilla fudge cake to Jaren. "I've got a question for you," he said.

That surprised her. He seemed more inclined *not* to ask any questions, and she was certain that he was given to the philosophy: the less you know about a person, the less likely you are to get close to that person.

"Okay," she responded, drawing the single word out.

Accepting the slice that Riley handed him, Kyle moved over to the side. Seeming to devote his attention to the cake on his plate, he asked, "Are you *always* this cheerful?"

There were times when a sadness threatened to overwhelm her, but she always fought it off. She'd seen what an innate sadness could do. It had eventually destroyed her father.

"I do my best."

"Well, stop it," Kyle ordered just before he took a bite of cake.

She glanced in his direction. There was a tolerant smile on her face that he found annoying and yet, still oddly attractive. Whatever else her faults were, she had an aura of sorts.

"You don't mean that," she replied. "You might think you do, but you don't."

"Oh, so now you think that you're a psychiatrist?" he scoffed.

"No, but I did take a few psych courses in college," she answered glibly. "Everyone is better off thinking positive than dwelling on the negative."

"I don't *dwell* on the negative," he corrected her tersely, "I accept reality for what it is."

"Or what you make it out to be," she countered.

"When I figure it out, I'll let you know," Kyle told her darkly and with that, he turned away and put distance between them. Her cheerfulness was *really* starting to get under his skin.

Feeling awkward was not something she ever allowed herself to experience for long. Left alone, Jaren made her way over to Andrew. The latter stood with his wife, Rose, as well as Callie, her husband and their children.

Callie smiled at her, then, excusing herself, she ushered her family away.

"What can I do for you, Jaren?" Andrew asked.

That he remembered her name amid all these other people, even if they were his family, told her the kind of man he was. She wondered if his family appreciated him.

"Chief, I just wanted to tell you that this has to be the best cake I've ever had."

Andrew allowed himself a moment to bask in the compliment. He knew exactly what he was capable of and had the utmost confidence in his abilities. But every once in a while, he relished hearing someone say it. His own family had become so accustomed to having their taste buds romanced. For the most part, the Cavanaughs took their meals here for granted.

"Thank you, Jaren. And it's Andrew," he corrected. "It hasn't been *Chief* for a very long time."

"If it's all the same to you, sir, I'd still like to call you Chief. You're my dad's age and it just doesn't seem respectful for me to call you by your first name."

He was nothing if not flexible. Raising five children single-handedly while searching for his missing wife had gone a long way in teaching him how to bend. "Then *Chief* it is," Andrew allowed kindly. As he spoke, he refilled her plate with another slice. "So, tell me, how long have you been in Aurora?"

It began simply enough, with her answering his question. That led to another question and another after that. Before she realized what was happening, Jaren found herself pouring out her heart to this man who had once known her father.

By the time she finished, Jaren confided to Andrew that his was a family that most people dreamed of having.

Andrew grinned broadly, surveying the room. "Yes, they did turn out pretty well, didn't they? And the most amazing part was that every last one of them found soul mates who blended well into this mix." He thought of the events of the last few months. "And just recently, the family expanded again when we gained Brian's four stepchildren, plus my late brother's trio." He glanced over his shoulder toward the room where he spent a good deal of his time each day—the kitchen. "We've had to expand the basic table that's in the kitchen. Again," he added with a soft chuckle.

"Not to mention that the kitchen's been expanded twice," Rose Cavanaugh told her, then confided, "You'd think with all that extra room, the man would let me in once in a while to experiment."

Andrew kissed the top of Rose's head, the deep affection he had for her evident in his eyes. "Experiment's the word for it all right," he agreed, humor curving the sides of his mouth. "I love you with all my heart, Rose, you know that, but you have to face the fact that you really can't boil water."

Rose gave an indifferent shrug. "I guess it's lucky for me, then, that I found you," she quipped.

"Very lucky," he agreed. The wink he gave her separated them from the rest of the room, creating their own little haven.

Wow, Jaren thought as she quietly stepped back to give the chief and his wife a private moment. After all these years, the two were still very much in love.

Maybe if her mother had felt that way about her

father, he might have still been around rather than seeking to decimate his liver a lethal ounce at a time.

But then, she reminded herself, her mother had initially left because of her father's drinking. Nora Rosetti's departure hadn't been the cause of her father's descent into the bottle. That had come about because of his inability to deal with the realities of his job, among other things—things that he took with him to the grave.

"Kind of makes you believe in love, doesn't it?"

Startled, Jaren turned around to see a young woman standing almost at her elbow. The woman bore a striking resemblance to Kyle.

"Yes," Jaren said with a sigh, "it does."

The young woman extended her hand to her. "Hi, I'm Greer O'Brien. Or Cavanaugh. I haven't quite decided yet," she admitted honestly. Her smile widened. "I hear you're my brother's new partner."

"I am," Jaren answered. Her curiosity piqued, she couldn't help asking, "Are you getting married to a Cavanaugh?"

Greer laughed. "No, turns out I am one. As are my brothers." Not nearly as private a creature as Kyle, Greer focused on the positive side of this latest development. "All information the three of us received via a deathbed confession from my mother."

Kyle had mentioned his mother's passing. But she'd had no idea that it had been this traumatic. "Oh, I'm sorry. I just recently lost my dad."

"Stings, doesn't it?" Jaren nodded in response. "It's

even worse when you find out that the parent you wor-shipped was keeping things back from you."

She could see why that would hurt. In the woman's shoes, she would have had trouble dealing with that herself. She tried to think of a reason that might be ac-ceptable to Kyle's sister.

"Maybe your mother was just afraid that you'd think badly of her if you knew the truth," she suggested. "From what I hear, parents care deeply what their chil-dren think of them."

The look in Greer's blue eyes told Jaren that she hadn't entertained that idea previously.

"Maybe you have something there," Greer com-mented, rolling the idea over in her head. And then she flashed a quick smile. "Makes it a little easier to deal with," she admitted. "But Mom should have known we wouldn't have sat in judgment of her."

That terrain was sensitive. And there no longer was a way to ever resolve this, now that her mother was gone. "Maybe she wasn't all that sure about Kyle," Jaren speculated.

A knowing look came into Greer's eyes. "How long did you say you've been my brother's partner?"

"This is my first day."

And rather than run off screaming, she had come here with Kyle. To a family gathering. There just might be hope for her brother yet, Greer thought. God knew she'd come close to giving up on him more than once.

"You just might last," Greer told her, a glimmer of

admiration in her very blue eyes. She pulled out a card from her pocket. "Here, this is my cell number on the bottom. Feel free to call me if he gets to be too much of a pain in the butt for you."

Although she'd been fighting her own battles now most of her life, Jaren decided to play along. There was no need to turn Greer down and hurt her feelings.

Taking the card, Jaren tucked it away in her pocket. "Thanks. I just might take you up on that."

She liked them, Jaren thought as she watched Greer weave her way back into the crowd. She liked each and every one of the Cavanaughs that she'd met.

That was reason enough for her to be determined to make her partnership work. The challenge would help her get over the gnawing loneliness that she sometimes felt inside when she considered her own situation. Alone was a terrible way to be.

"Thanks for letting me tag along last night," Jaren said to her partner the following morning as they headed out to begin the first wave of interviews with the dead neurosurgeon's patients.

He hated to be thanked, hated to be in the position of having someone feel beholden to him. It made him as uncomfortable as hell.

"No big deal. You looked like you had a rough day and could stand some good food. It's no secret that Andrew enjoys taking people under his wing."

Jaren noticed that he talked about her rough day as if he wasn't responsible for it. But then, maybe bringing her with him to the birthday party had been his way of making up for it.

In either case, she wasn't about to get into a discussion with him about that, certainly not first thing in the morning. They needed a good working relationship in place before she felt confident enough to raise contrary points. So instead, she merely smiled appreciatively. After all, Kyle O'Brien was certainly under no obligation to make any kind of amends.

"The Cavanaughs seem like really nice people," she commented.

Getting into his Crown Victoria, he waited for her to get in on the passenger side. "They're a decent lot," he allowed.

Jaren wondered if that was a ringing endorsement in *Kyle-speak*. Getting in, she buckled up and adjusted the shoulder strap.

"I met your sister. Greer," she added in case he thought she was talking about his half sister, Patience. "She told me that she was debating changing her last name."

Although he was grateful for the hospitality that Andrew Cavanaugh and his younger brother, Brian, had shown him and his siblings, Kyle felt it was a little too early in the game to think about changing the name on the top of his dance card.

"Yeah, well, Greer always was the one who was quick to forgive and forget."

"But you're not like that?" She raised her voice as he started the car. The question was rhetorical.

"Like I told you, I'm a realist." His tone tabled the discussion.

They drove the rest of the way in relative silence—his, not hers. Nothing, he was beginning to believe, stopped this woman from chatting away. He missed his old partner more than ever. The two of them could spend almost the entire day in silence and it didn't get old.

Pulling up to a closed gate, Kyle identified himself and his partner to the disembodied voice that came over the callbox. The gates parted and they drove on through until they reached the building in the distance.

The word *mansion* would have been an understatement, he thought, bringing the sedan to a halt in the winding driveway. This was home, or at least one of them, for Jackson Massey, the wealthy founder of Massey Enterprises, a corporation that had holdings in a dozen and a half international companies around the globe.

"Wonder what it costs to run this place," Jaren murmured.

"Like the man said, if you have to ask, you can't afford it." Kyle rang the bell and heard what sounded like a funeral dirge come through the door. A moment later, the door was opened by a solemn-faced older woman with white hair and a pale complexion.

Kyle held up his ID. "Detectives O'Brien and Rosetti to see Jackson Massey. Is he in, ma'am?"

"No, Mr. Jackson's not in," the housekeeper replied, her voice quavering.

"When will he be in?" Kyle pressed.

"Never, I'm afraid." The woman paused to dab at her eyes. A huge sigh escaped her lips. "Mr. Jackson's gone," she added.

"Gone?" Kyle echoed. Dr. Barrett's former patient had houses and offices all over the world. Had he decided to suddenly move? "Gone where?" he asked her.

"Why, to God, of course. Mr. Jackson died a little more than a week ago," the housekeeper answered, her eyes welling up. Tears began to slide down the soft face.

Well, that gave Jackson Massey an airtight alibi, Kyle thought. But he believed in tying up loose ends. "Is there anyone in his family we could speak to?"

The woman pressed her lips together, clearly struggling to regain control over herself. "There's Mr. Finley, his son. But I'm not sure if he's up to having visitors."

"We'll be quick," Jaren promised. It earned her an annoyed look from Kyle, but her reassurance seemed to put the housekeeper at ease.

The woman took a deep breath before nodding. "All right, but please be gentle with him. Mr. Finley's always been rather fragile."

Following the housekeeper through the huge residence that could have easily contained several families whose paths never crossed, Jaren turned toward Kyle. "Would you like me to handle this?" she offered. "No disrespect intended, but I really don't see you having the patience to coddle someone."

He didn't bother disputing that with her. He had plenty of patience, but not when it came to men with no backbones. Besides, it might be interesting to see the woman in action.

"Go ahead," he told her. "Let's see what you're made of."

Finley Massey was in the study. Grief over his father's death had left his eyes red-rimmed and his wheat-colored hair in disarray. Of medium height and slight build, he appeared to have slept in his clothes and gave the impression of a man struggling to rise above his grief with only partial success.

Greeting them, Finley apologized for his appearance. He gestured for them to take a seat on the sofa, then proceeded to answer their questions.

"Your father was one of Dr. Barrett's patients," Jaren began.

"He was," Finley replied, a haunted look in the man's bloodshot eyes.

There was no genteel way to put this. "Dr. Barrett was found murdered in his office yesterday."

"Murdered?" Finley repeated, as if chewing on the word. "What happened?"

"That's what we're trying to piece together," she said, deliberately omitting the detail about the stake being driven through the surgeon's heart. Finley Massey didn't look as if he could handle that kind of information well. He'd paled at the mention of the surgeon's murder.

"Maybe it was karma," Finley volunteered.

"Karma?" Kyle asked uncertainly.

Finley nodded. "He wasn't a very nice man. Despite his exorbitant fees, he acted as if he was doing you a favor by taking on your case. He wasn't very nice to my father. His receptionist told me he was like that with everyone." He blew out a breath, as if talking tired him. "Maybe someone took offense at his attitude."

"It's possible," Kyle agreed.

Several times during the short interview, Massey's son appeared to drift away. This was, he explained, his father's study and contained a great many memories for him.

"I wish you could have known him. He was larger than life," Finley said proudly. "And I'm not ashamed to say that he was always my hero." He looked down at his hands. "I'm not sure just how to get along without him."

"Take it one day at a time," Jaren advised. "It's all you can do."

"I suppose you're right." Finley sighed, then glanced up from his folded hands. "Are there any other questions I can answer for you?"

"None that we can think of right now," Kyle replied, rising. "If we do, we'll be in touch."

The minute they walked out, Jaren eyed her partner. "Where do I know his name from?"

"Jackson Massey? He was a big deal with—"

"No," she stopped him. "I mean his son. Finley Massey. His name is really familiar. Like I've heard it or read it somewhere before." Jaren pressed her lips together, thinking as they walked back to the car. And then she shrugged. "It's probably nothing," she admitted. "But I know that it's going to drive me crazy until I remember where I came across it and figure it out."

Kyle spared her a look. She'd be the one to know about crazy, he thought. "Welcome to the club," he murmured.

# Chapter 5

The following day, Kyle and Jaren were walking away from their first interview of the morning when his cell rang.

Digging the phone out of his pocket, he flipped it open. "O'Brien."

Lengthening her stride to keep up, Jaren slanted a glance at her partner. It was impossible to gauge the conversation just by looking at his face. The man had to be one hell of a poker player, she surmised. She stopped next to the passenger side of the car.

"No, we're not that far away. Right. We should be able to get there within the half hour."

"What's up?" she asked the second he ended the conversation. She had to wait until he closed his phone and slipped it back into his pocket.

Opening his door, Kyle got in behind the steering wheel. "Looks like vampire slaying seems to be in season."

Jaren was quick to get in. "Come again?"

"Someone found the chairman of the board of Massey Enterprises in his corporate suite this morning. Edward Cummings was lying on the floor—"

"—With a stake driven through his heart?" Jaren cried in disbelief.

Turning his key in the ignition, Kyle pulled away from the curb. "Not much on letting people finish their sentences, are you?"

Jaren let his comment slide. Something a lot bigger was going on here. She tried to wrap her mind around the concept. Everyone talked about serial killers, but in actuality, they were relatively rare. This killer had the makings of one.

"Do you think that we have a serial killer on our hands?"

Kyle laughed shortly as he got onto the freeway ramp. "What, a vampire slayer?" he asked, repeating the term he'd glibly used.

His tone made it sound like a grade B movie made around a forgotten comic book or video game. "Not a real vampire slayer, there's no such thing," she said, in case he thought she believed in something so preposterous. "But if the M.O. is the same…"

Kyle refused to go down that road. He tended to be conservative in his thinking. Less mistakes that way and less embarrassment.

"Most likely, whoever did this read about the first

murder in the paper and decided to make use of the publicity—which is why I have absolutely no use for the media," he added with feeling. Signaling, he sped up and got in front of a produce truck. "Or maybe the same person killed both, but only wanted to kill one of them and used the other for cover," he theorized.

Stranger things had happened and that was still more likely than jumping to the conclusion that a deranged serial killer was loose, determined to rid the world of vampires.

Sitting back in her seat, Jaren exhaled. Her mind was going in twelve different directions at once. Both O'Brien's theories made sense, as did her own thoughts on the matter.

"Hell of a lot of possibilities," she murmured more to herself than to Kyle.

"You think?"

She wasn't sure if he was agreeing with her, or mocking her. But something had just occurred to her and right now was no time to take offense. That was for after the case was solved.

"You think this might be a coincidence?"

There she went again, plucking out nothing out of the middle without a proper preamble. He didn't know what was worse, her talking all the time, or her beginning in the middle of a thought.

"What's a coincidence?"

"That the head of Massey Enterprises died last week and now the chairman of the board of directors gets killed? Do you think that someone might have it in for Massey Enterprises?"

"Jackson Massey died of complications from his surgery," Kyle reminded her. "This latest victim died of complications arising from having a stake driven through his heart. Besides, what you're suggesting doesn't take the doctor's murder into account—"

"It might if the doctor suspected something was wrong, or had uncovered criminal activity at Massey Enterprises and had started asking questions."

"Why don't you hold off coming up with any more theories until we get a look at the scene of the crime?"

"Okay." Jaren did her best to curb her outward enthusiasm, but there was no way she could properly curb her mind, which continued examining the possibilities.

The second they entered the incredibly spacious, 1800-square-foot suite that belonged to the chairman of the Massey Enterprises' board of directors, Kyle felt his breath back up in his lungs.

"What is that smell?" He looked around for the source and then stopped dead. Someone had thrown up next to the body.

A short, dark-haired man in an off-green jumpsuit that identified him as one of the building's cleaning crew was on his knees, wiping away the visual display of Edward Cummings's personal assistant's weak stomach. Roxanne Smith had been the one who'd walked into the suite this morning and found the body.

"Hold it right there," Kyle called out to the man as he pulled on a pair of rubber gloves. Small dark eyes looked up at him quizzically. "Don't touch anything else," Kyle instructed.

"Okay," the man replied meekly. He rose to his feet and stepped aside, waiting for further orders.

Jaren looked at him in surprise. "You think CSI is going to want to process vomit?"

"CSI processes everything. It's a simple give-and-take relationship. I don't tread on their feet, they don't tread on mine," he told her. "And everyone gets along."

The man really was full of surprises. "I didn't think you cared about getting along."

Scanning the spacious office, Kyle made a few notes to himself, then flipped the small notepad closed. "When it helps solve a case, I can be the soul of cooperation."

She'd believe that when she saw it, Jaren thought. "Call my attention to it when it happens, please. I'd like to film that for posterity."

She'd gotten pretty damn cocky in the three days she'd been with the department, he thought. He hadn't made up his mind whether it irritated the hell out of him, or amused him.

Most likely, it was a little of both, he decided. "Who found the body?" he asked one of the two officers on the premises.

"The chairman's assistant. According to her, the chairman likes to have his coffee waiting for him when he arrives at exactly nine o'clock."

"A little anal," Kyle commented.

"But punctual," Jaren added.

"Always the bright side," Kyle muttered under his breath. "Where is this assistant?"

"At her desk," the officer replied, pointing to one of the three doors that led out of the suite.

Roxanne Smith had been at her job longer than the now-deceased chairman. Thin, with understated makeup and a subdued brown suit, the assistant was still visibly shaking. Her hands were clasped tightly in her lap in an effort to still them. So far, she was failing.

"I'm sorry. I never saw a dead person before." She looked from Kyle to Jaren, bewilderment in her eyes. "Who would want to do such a gruesome thing?"

"That's what we were hoping you could tell us," Jaren said kindly. "Did Cummings have any enemies?"

Roxanne swallowed to hold back the tears. "Of course he had enemies. He was a rich, powerful man. You don't get to be the chairman of the board of such a large corporation without making a few enemies." And then, because she seemed afraid of generating the wrong impression about her late boss, she quickly added, "But most of the people he worked with liked Mr. Cummings. As far as CEOs went, he was fairer than most."

Roxanne shivered and it was obvious that she struggled to hold herself together. "I'm going to have nightmares about this for the rest of my life," she wailed.

"Is there anyone we can call for you? A relative, a spouse, a friend?" Jaren offered.

Roxanne shook her head as she ran her hands up and down her arms, attempting to stave off a bone-deep chill. And then suddenly, a look of renewed anxiety surfaced. "Someone has to tell Mrs. Cummings."

"We'll take care of that," Kyle told her matter-of-factly.

"According to what we heard, he was pretty punctual, arriving at nine each morning. Do you have any idea what he was doing in the office early?" Jaren asked.

There was confusion in the assistant's eyes. "He wasn't early. That was the suit he wore last night."

Jaren exchanged looks with Kyle. Had the man been entertaining someone after hours and the visit had gone sour? But then, they were back to the stake through the heart M.O. Would a woman have the strength to do that?

"Do you feel up to giving us a formal statement?" Jaren asked the woman kindly.

Roxanne pressed her lips together and nodded. Her breath was shaky when she released it. "Yes, I—I think so."

"Good, I'd like you to go with this officer," Jaren beckoned over the policeman who was closest to her, "and tell him everything you can think of that happened last night before you left." Jaren raised her eyes to the tall officer. "Would you mind taking Ms. Smith's statement, please?"

It was a rhetorical question, but the officer nodded in compliance. For a flicker of a second, a grin curved his mouth until he seemed to realize that his reaction was totally out of sync with what was going on. He sobered quickly.

As she ushered the personal assistant toward the officer, Jaren glanced toward Kyle. Her partner was silently watching her. It didn't take her long to realize why.

She'd usurped him. Again.

"I'm doing it again, aren't I?" It wasn't intended as a real question. "I'm sorry. I'm used to being the primary on cases," she confessed. "It's going to take a little adjusting for me to hold back."

He watched her for another long moment, his eyes holding hers. He couldn't picture her in a position of authority. Just what kind of a homicide division did they have back in Oakland? And then he said, "Work on it."

"Absolutely," she promised.

Kyle squatted down beside the body to get a closer look at the victim and the wooden stake that had ended his life. He'd just begun his hands-off survey when he heard the M.E. arriving. In his wake were the other crime-scene investigators.

Wayne Carter had opted to become a medical examiner because the patients on his table didn't argue with him, and didn't challenge his rulings. He felt the peace and quiet was worth the knowledge that he would never be able to cure anyone.

Walking into the suite, the M.E. wrinkled his large Roman nose. "What *is* that smell?"

"Something we hope your people'll process quickly." Kyle addressed his remark to Hank Elder, the CSI team leader who entered directly behind the M.E.

Dr. Carter sighed when he got a good look at the latest victim.

"Another stake through the heart?" He looked up at Kyle. "Has everyone lost their minds?"

"Looks that way." Kyle rose to his feet. As he did so,

he noted that Jaren had gone wandering through the room. She seemed to be taking everything in, like the personification of a mobile, roving camera. "Anything strike your fancy, Rosetti?" Kyle asked, raising his voice.

"Come here," she requested in a subdued tone that seemed completely out of character for her.

Jaren was standing by the chairman's desk. A number of papers were scattered about, but in general it appeared rather neat. Which was why Jaren saw it. The book that lay on the corner of the desk looked out of place.

"What?" Kyle demanded impatiently.

"You have to see this," she told him. And then she turned around to see if he was coming. "Guess what Cummings was reading?"

That got Kyle's attention. Because of the stake through the man's heart, he immediately thought of the book they'd found in the surgeon's office.

Kyle was at her side in a minimum number of steps. "You're kidding."

Jaren shook her head. She held up the bestseller. "I never kid about a murder."

He took the book from her and looked at the cover in disbelief. "This is a hell of a way to get publicity for a book," he commented.

She looked at him, stunned. "You don't really think the author is behind this?"

"One thing I've learned is that you don't rule out anything automatically. But it would be pretty stupid of him—"

"Her," Jaren corrected.

He looked down at the book he was holding. "It says 'Mackenzie Carrey' on the cover."

Jaren smiled. She had a feeling that he was only tuned in to police work. Everything outside of that, including pop culture, didn't exist for him. "In this case, Mackenzie is a woman."

He merely sighed and shook his head. "All right, whatever. Right now, we'll go see Mrs. Cummings and go from there."

"So, we're finished here for now?" she asked.

He glanced toward Cummings's assistant. The woman appeared a little more composed than she had a few minutes ago. "See if you can get a list from his assistant of people Cummings might have stepped on in his ascent to the top."

"I'm on it," she said, crossing to Roxanne Smith's desk.

Unlike the neurosurgeon's ex-wife, Jane Cummings all but came unglued right before their eyes when she finally accepted the fact that this wasn't some elaborate hoax that her husband, a habitual practical joker, had instigated.

Jaren sat down beside the woman, putting her arm around her as if she were a friend. Watching her, Kyle silently acknowledged that he didn't have that kind of capability. He'd always had trouble relating to people, preferring to keep a safe emotional distance between himself and them. Made things far less complicated.

"Did your husband do that often?" Kyle finally asked Mrs. Cummings when her sobs had quieted down. "Play practical jokes?"

She nodded. The tissue in her hands was completely shredded. Jaren leaned over and pulled another out of the box on the coffee table. She handed it to the woman.

"I used to tell him that they'd backfire on him someday. Edward would only laugh. But he had been tapering off this last year, hoping to present a more serious image of himself to Mr. Massey."

"Because he'd been promoted to chairman?" Jaren guessed. The woman nodded. Fresh tears gathered in her eyes.

"With your husband gone, who's next in line?" Kyle asked.

Jane Cummings looked up at him blankly and shook her head. "I don't know," she admitted, her voice hollow. "Edward never liked me asking about his work. Said as long as his position fulfilled my every wish, I didn't need to be made aware of all the tedious details." The thin, angular woman shrugged, as if the arrangement had been fine with her. "I don't really have a head for business, anyway. Oh, God." Jane Cummings covered her mouth with her hands to keep back a fresh sob as a new thought occurred to her. A frantic look entered her eyes. "What am I going to tell the children?"

"How old are they?" Jaren asked.

Dazed, it took the woman a moment to remember. She looked, Jaren thought, as if she was going into shock. "Matthew is ten and Edward, Jr. is twelve."

"Try to break it to them as gently as possible. The

media is going to be all over this by the evening news," Jaren warned her.

"The media?" Jane repeated numbly, as if her thoughts hadn't taken her that far yet.

"Are you aware that Dr. Barrett was killed in the exact same fashion?" Kyle asked.

The expression on her face told them that he might as well have pulled any name out of the air. "Dr. Barrett?" she repeated without comprehension.

"Richard Barrett," Kyle elaborated, studying her face. Either the woman was an accomplished actress, or she really had never heard the name before. "Did your husband know him?"

She shook her head. "I don't know. He knew a lot of people, but we never entertained the man socially. I do know that there was no Dr. Barrett on the board. I know all the people on the board." Fresh tears were sliding down her cheeks again. "They come to our parties," she explained.

They remained with Mrs. Cummings a little longer, asking a few more questions. But for now, Kyle decided that they'd gotten as far with the woman as they could. She wasn't telling them anything that shed any light on the crime.

She did, however, give them one piece of information that could possibly be relevant. The bestseller they took from Cummings's desk belonged to her, not him. She'd met her husband for lunch yesterday afternoon and had accidentally left the book behind.

Because of the way Cummings had been killed, Mrs.

Cummings looked nervously from Jaren to Kyle. "You don't think that book had anything to do with my husband being killed, do you?"

"No, of course not," Jaren was quick to assure her. "We're just tying up loose ends, that's all."

They left Jane Cummings sitting on her sofa, looking more like a lost child than the wife of the late head of one of the most influential corporations in the country.

"You seemed pretty sure of yourself back there," Kyle commented as they walked out of the custom-built house. "Saying the book had nothing to do with it. Changed your mind about it?"

"No, I still think there's some kind of connection. What I said was for her benefit—and for her kids. If that woman thought that her leaving the book behind was in any way responsible for her husband's death, she would have completely fallen apart." Jaren found herself heading for the driver's side. Habit, she thought, retracing her steps and coming around to the passenger side. "So, until we find out otherwise, why make her suffer?"

He thought of his old partner. Rosatti didn't have a thing in common with Castle. Compassion had never been one of the retired detective's failings. As for him, well, he found that compassion could get in the way.

"Just what made you become a cop?" he asked out of the blue as he got into the vehicle.

She thought for a moment. "My father was a cop and I like helping people."

He didn't look at his job that way. He thought of it

as a chance to put away the bad guys. "You're a little too touchy-feely for this kind of work, don't you think?"

She gave him one of those smiles that were beginning to get under his skin and definitely on his nerves. "The way I see it, people like me balance out people like you."

He decided it was better all around if he just kept silent as they drove to interview the first name on the list of people Cummings's assistant had given them. He knew a no-win situation when he saw one.

There was no shortage of people to talk to. Most of the people on the list Roxanne Smith had put together had an alibi for the previous evening. The ones who didn't went on a short list that Kyle thought was none too promising.

No tangible connection existed between the two murders, other than the method used and the book found at both crime scenes. Initially, Kyle had guessed that the killer was leaving a calling card. But since the second book had belonged to the victim's wife, that possibility was ruled out.

They saw twelve more people that day, some connected to the neurosurgeon, some to Cummings.

They even went back to reinterview Finley Massey since his father had founded the corporation that Cummings had briefly headed, but Jackson Massey's heir could shed no more light on the chairman's murder than he could on the surgeon's. About the only information the younger man could offer was to point them to the next possible successor to the deceased Cummings.

"How about you?" Kyle asked Finley before they left. "Don't you figure into the setup somehow?"

Finley laughed as if the idea struck him as absurd.

"I just cash the checks when they come. My father was the thinker, the one who could make things work. He always called me the dreamer." When he spoke of his father, there was a fond note in his voice, a softness that was hard to miss. "He didn't want me in the business. He wanted me to find my own destiny, said he didn't care what I was doing or what I became, as long as I was happy." There was the soft sheen of unshed tears as he looked at them and concluded, "He was that kind of a man."

"And were you?" Jaren asked. "Happy?" she added when he didn't answer.

"I was." There was a heaviness in his voice, a sadness that sounded as if it would never leave. "Until he died. Now I'm not sure I'll ever be able to find my way again. He was my compass."

Jaren's heart went out to Finley. She knew what it was like to feel alone.

# Chapter 6

They were asking too many questions.

Were they agents sent to lure him out and kill him the way they couldn't all those years ago? They would have succeeded back then, if it hadn't been for his Protector.

*The Protector didn't come in time to save you, D, but he saved me.*

But now, there was no one. Not the Protector, not D. No one.

He was alone and defenseless. Who would be there to save him when they came again?

And they would come. They already had. They'd killed his Protector and they would kill him. Unless he killed them first.

Oh, but there were so many of them. So very many. For each one he destroyed, another came.

He had to keep fighting.

With a deep, shuddering sigh, he looked out at the darkness beyond the window. This was their time.

He was tempted to stay inside and bar the doors. But they would find a way to get in. To get at him.

He had to keep moving.

To fool them.

To stay alive until the dawn so that he could be safe for another day.

They were afraid of the light. His Protector had told him so when he'd rescued him.

Even though it was dark, he needed to get out. To clear his head. To think even though it was getting harder and harder to do. Thoughts didn't want to penetrate the wall of pain that wrapped around him.

It was almost unbearable.

Arming himself against the forces that seemed always just a heartbeat away, he went out the front door.

Praying.

Jaren simply didn't remember closing her eyes—she really didn't.

The last thing she recalled was staring at the chart she'd compiled. A chart comparing the two victims' vital statistics. She grew steadily disheartened because she found far more differences between the two than commonalities. The only thing that linked the two victims was that both had higher degrees from prominent universities. And both were worth a great deal of money.

Was that what it was about? Jaren couldn't help wondering as she struggled to focus. Money? Was there someone out there with a vendetta against rich people in this time of tense economic strife?

But then why these two men and not some other two? she silently asked as she looked at the photographs she'd laid side by side.

And what in heaven's name did the stake through the heart mean? It had to mean something. People just weren't killed that way.

Jaren spent the better part of the night trying to wrap her mind around the question or more precisely, the lack of an answer. And then suddenly, she found herself tuning in on a sharp ache at the back of her neck. A cottony, sickeningly sweet taste exploded in her mouth and an annoying noise came from directly behind her.

Lifting her head, Jaren discovered that she was the not-so-proud owner of a killer headache shooting out from her jaw to the top of her head via her right temple.

She also found she could place the annoying noise. It came from Kyle.

Somehow, it had gotten to be morning without her knowing it.

As she blinked away the cobwebs from her eyes, she saw Kyle moving around to stand directly in front of her. The detective was laying claim to a section of her desk with his very tight butt.

When had she noticed that he had one of those?

"Didn't you go home last night?" Kyle asked, looking at her face.

She didn't respond right away. Feeling just this side of warmed-over death, she took a breath, then asked him, "What time is it?"

"Eight."

"In the morning?" It was a rhetorical question. The sun had moved into the squad room full force, causing her to squint.

"Yes," Kyle answered patiently.

"Then I guess I didn't." Why was he asking her dumb questions?

Shifting so that several parts of her back whispered protesting noises, Jaren took another deep breath and then looked down at the papers and photographs spread out haphazardly on her desk. She'd slept on two of them and was fairly sure they'd left their imprint on her cheek.

She dragged her hand through her hair. "I was looking for some kind of connection between our victims and I guess time just got away from me."

"Did you find a connection?" he asked, pretty certain he knew the answer. If she had found one, she would have called him no matter what time it was. It was just something that he sensed about her.

Jaren shook her head, fighting off a feeling of frustration. "Not unless being rich is a connection."

Kyle tried not to notice how her hair seemed to swing back and forth rhythmically. And hypnotically.

"Some recently laid-off person taking out his frustrations on strangers?" he guessed. "Might have worked if our killer had indiscriminately sprayed the crowd with a shotgun, but he didn't. He picked them out one by one and then drove a stake through their hearts." Kyle looked down at the two photographs, each taken at the scene of the crime. They were chilling and yet macabrely comical at the same time. "Some nerd trying to make the world safe from vampires?"

"Right, that'll fly in court," Jaren cracked wearily.

She ran her hand along the back of her neck, trying to will away the crick she felt there. The next moment, she stiffened as Kyle's strong fingers moved beneath her hand and began kneading the tight knots. She tried to turn around and found she couldn't. He had *very* strong fingers.

"What are you doing?" she demanded.

"Being nice?" He made his answer sound like a question.

Jaren managed to pull back, shifting her chair around quickly so that she wound up facing him. She pushed aside his hand. "I'm okay."

He made no attempt to continue to massage her. "The jury's still out about that one." Straightening, he moved over to his own desk. "You look like hell, Rosetti. Why don't you go home and catch a few hours' sleep? I'll cover for you."

That was all she needed, to go home at the start of the day. She knew how it would look, accepting preferential treatment after being here only a few days. Her butt would be out on the street in a matter of hours.

"Thanks," she said icily. "But I don't need covering."

Woman was too stubborn for her own good, Kyle

thought. That gave her a lot in common with Greer. "Don't you have a dog or something at your place, waiting to be fed?" he prodded. She'd do him no good dead on her feet.

"No," she answered crisply. "There's nothing waiting for me at my place."

Which was one of the reasons she'd opted to work on the case after everyone else had gone home. As the last of the detectives had taken their leave, the precinct slipped into a soft silence. There was an aura of safety about it that made her feel good as well as warm. There was no such feeling at the apartment yet. There might never be.

Kyle looked at her in surprise. "You're kidding. I thought for sure you were the dog-waiting-at-the-door-for-the-sound-of-mistress's-footsteps type."

She laughed softly, shaking her head. "Sorry to disappoint you. No dog." And then she paused for a moment, debating whether or not to say anything further. She decided it would do no harm. "I had a dog," she finally admitted.

He could tell by the sound of her voice that he'd accidentally opened up an old wound. "What happened to him?"

"*She* died," Jaren answered, purposely emphasizing the animal's gender. Why was it that everyone automatically assumed that all dogs were males and all cats were females? Propagation would have come to a screeching standstill long ago if that scenario were even remotely the case. "Less than a week after my father passed away."

"I'm really sorry to hear that."

Jaren shrugged carelessly, as if Annabelle's death had made no difference to her. As if she hadn't cried the entire night after finding the Yorkie's rigid little body on the kitchen floor. "All just part of life, right?"

"So they tell me," Kyle allowed. "But I can still be sorry."

She didn't want his sympathy—or pity. "That is your God-given right," she agreed flippantly, her tone closing the subject. Standing up, she unconsciously stretched, then caught Kyle smiling as his eyes washed over the length of her. The expression in his eyes both annoyed her and warmed her. "Look, give me a few minutes and I'll be ready to roll."

His desk was littered with work and as far as he knew, they had questioned everyone connected to one or the other of the two victims. "Are we rolling?" Kyle asked innocently.

Before she could say anything in response to the assumption she'd made, the lieutenant stuck his head out of his office.

"O'Brien, Rosetti, you're up."

At this point, that could only mean one thing. They both turned toward their superior.

"Another one?" Kyle asked before Jaren had a chance to.

The lieutenant nodded. "Another one," he echoed, then rattled off the address as he crossed to them. The location wasn't that far away. The man handed Kyle the notepaper he'd used when he'd taken down the information just now.

"Guess the coffee'll have to wait," Jaren said more to herself than to Kyle. She really needed coffee in the morning. Nothing strong, just hot and sweet. But she'd get by, she told herself.

"We'll pick some up on the way," Kyle promised, grabbing the jacket he'd just shed a moment ago. He pulled it back on as he led the way out of the squad room.

"So much for my theory about a rage against rich people," Jaren said with a sigh as she squatted down beside the newest victim.

The coffee Kyle got for both of them had more than done the trick. Nine parts caffeine, one part liquid, it brought every nerve ending in her body to attention. Overtired and wired, her body was at war with itself. But all that went on hold the moment she had approached the inert body of the latest victim.

From initial appearances, the so-called vampire slayer's newest victim was a homeless man. And not just any homeless man, but one who had gained a small bit of notoriety over the last few years. The dead man had a long, flowing gray-white beard. His skin was the color of aged parchment, yellowed long before its time by a harsh sun and an even harsher environment.

But the most noticeable thing about the victim was the dark, flowing cape that he wore over his black, shabby clothing. Winter, summer, no matter what the weather or the season, the Count, as he had been dubbed by an amused journalist who had once done a human-interest story on the man, always wore his cape. With his broad shoulders and his body almost in constant movement—like a symphony that would not end—the Count gave the appearance of being larger than he actually was.

He didn't look so large right now, Kyle thought, looking down at the lifeless man.

The Count lay in an alley behind one of the restaurants he was given to frequenting. Busboys and swing-shift cooks would feel sorry for him and set aside leftovers for the man, which was one of the reasons the Count looked so well fed rather than gaunt. He didn't sing for his supper, but in exchange for the leftovers, the Count would spin entertaining, elaborate stories about his life as a citizen of the night. No one ever took the man seriously.

"You know," Jaren said thoughtfully as she rose up to her feet again, still eyeing the victim, "this one actually looks the part."

"What part?" Kyle asked.

"Of a vampire."

"So, you're saying someone's going around, thinking they're killing vampires." The whole thing sounded even more ludicrous out loud.

She waved a hand at the body. The cape was twisted around the Count like a cocoon. At a quick glance, it looked as if he was attempting to undulate his way out of it.

"Certainly looks that way," Jaren said, "but I'm open to a better theory. You got one?"

Kyle shook his head. "Not at the moment," he sighed.

And then he shook his head angrily. "Damn it, the Count never hurt anyone."

Her eyes widened as she glanced at her partner. "You knew him?" That hadn't occurred to her.

"Everybody *knew* him," he told Jaren. "At least by sight. He's been hanging around this area for years." To his knowledge, the Count moved around a four-block square area, making it his domain.

"You keep calling him *the Count*. What's his real name?"

Kyle shrugged. "Haven't got a clue. Neither did he, I think."

If the Count had a family, as far as he knew, the man never mentioned them. He'd stopped to buy the man a meal or give him money for one on several occasions. And never once had he seen or heard of the Count imbibing anything alcoholic. He was just a poor, disoriented man who never did anyone any harm. Kyle couldn't help wondering if his death meant anything to anyone. *Did* he have a family looking for him even now?

"We can have his prints run through the system, see if he's a government employee or former military man." Give him a name in death even if he never used one in life, Kyle thought.

"His thumb print might give us a driver's license and a former address," Jaren suggested. "It would be a start."

A start. It was a little late for that, Kyle thought. But he nodded in response to her suggestion. "Everything but a reason why he's lying here like that and why someone would have wanted to kill him like some comic-book character."

Jaren made no comment. Instead, she squatted down again beside the body, taking care not to accidentally step into the blood that pooled beneath him. Behind her, the CSI unit was just arriving.

Her attention was focused on the stake that had been used. It looked identical to the other two stakes. "What kind of wood is this?" she asked Kyle.

Kyle looked over her shoulder. Damn if he knew.

"Sorry, but that's not within my field of expertise," he told her. He thought a moment. "But we can get someone at CSI to find out. Why?"

She was grasping at straws but straws were all they had. "If it's unusual, or found only in one place, then maybe it might lead us to the killer."

No harm in asking, he thought. "Worth a shot," Kyle agreed. And then he smiled at her. "Nice to know you can think on your feet."

"I'm lucky to be able to think at all," Jaren countered. She'd been feeling nauseous for the last twenty minutes. Ever since she'd finished her cup of coffee. "Where did you get that coffee from?" she asked.

"I picked it up at the coffee shop." And then he looked at her. "You were there. You saw me."

It had been more or less a rhetorical question. "You drink that on a regular basis?"

"Whenever I can. Why? What's wrong with it?"

He drank it and he had to ask? The only reason she'd consumed it was because she'd been hungry as well as thirsty and had hoped that the thick liquid would temporarily satisfy both needs.

"Nothing, if I had a huge pothole to fill," she told him, then added, "I've chewed on softer asphalt."

There was just no pleasing some people, he thought. Served him right for trying to do a good deed. "Next time, you pick up the coffee."

"I will," Jaren retorted, turning on her heel and walking away from him. She took exactly three steps before her conscience got the better of her. With a sigh, she turned around again to face him. "Sorry. I didn't mean to bite your head off. I tend to get cranky when I don't get enough sleep," she confessed.

"Thanks for the heads-up." There was just the slightest hint of sarcasm in Kyle's voice.

It was on the tip of Jaren's tongue to tell him what she thought of him *and* his crack. But that would only lead back into an argument and she was in no shape to hold up her end. So, rather than parry back, she swallowed her retort and continued to examine the scene of the crime.

This time, there was no copy of *The Vampire Diaries* left lying around. But in this case, it was obvious that the victim's appearance was more than enough to convey the message.

Someone was slaying vampires, whether real to the killer or just a sarcastic comment on something that was currently eluding the rest of them, Jaren didn't know. But they had to find this person and quickly because the ante seemed to have been stepped up. The time between slayings was decreasing.

They canvassed the immediate area to no avail.

No one had seen or heard anything. The Count had apparently died as silently as he had lived.

While the other two deaths might have had some kind of motive attributed to the executions, the Count's death mystified Kyle.

"As far as I know," he told Jaren, "other than being a little off his nut, the Count never offended anyone. Why would someone want to see him dead?" He posed the question as they drove back to the precinct.

"Maybe whoever did this didn't see him." Kyle spared her a quizzical glance as he made a right turn. "Maybe what the killer saw—or thought he saw—was a real vampire," she explained.

"You really believe that?" he asked incredulously. He'd tossed it out himself, but he'd been teasing.

She shrugged. "I believe everything until a theory is discounted. Most serial killers are off balance anyway."

"But why now?" he queried.

With a frustrated shrug, Jaren took a stab at it. "Maybe seeing *The Vampire Diaries* triggered him. Or maybe something happened in his personal life that set him off. All we have to do is find out what and we have our killer."

"*All,*" Kyle echoed with a short laugh.

She nodded her head. "I know. Pretty big word," she agreed. She just hoped that it wouldn't turn out to be too big for them to handle.

# Chapter 7

Bone weary and not wanting a repeat performance of last night, Jaren went home at the end of the day.

She called in an order at the pizzeria located in the center of the strip mall she'd just discovered the other morning. On her way home, she swung by the restaurant to pick up what was going to constitute her dinner as well as her breakfast for the next couple of days—one extra-large pizza.

The thin-crusted, extra-cheese-and-meat offering was still warm and resting on the passenger seat beside her, filling the interior of her small vehicle with a comforting aroma. She could almost feel her salivary glands kicking in and going into overdrive. She was tempted to take a piece and start eating as she drove, but she managed to refrain.

After bringing the pizza inside her second-floor garden apartment, Jaren deposited the large box on the kitchenette table. Determined to exercise control, Jaren went to change, putting on a pair of comfortable jeans and a T-shirt. On her way back to the kitchen, she turned on her TV set. The two things she'd done on the day she'd moved in was have the electricity turned on and have the cable company hook up her set.

The channel that came on now didn't matter. She kept the TV on for company, wanting something besides silence to fill the room. As she returned to the kitchen, Jaren also turned on most of the lights in the apartment.

Usually, the dark didn't bother her, but this case, with its eerie details, was getting under her skin. Until she could come to some kind of logical conclusion about the nature of the killer, she preferred seeing into all the corners of her apartment.

Not that that was an easy trick. There were towers of opened and unopened boxes scattered throughout the two-bedroom apartment. She'd been in Aurora a full two weeks now and so far, she'd only unpacked necessities.

Admittedly, Jaren thought ruefully, she wasn't much of a housekeeper these days, but then, those weren't the skills that the police department required of her. Her years of caring for her father, of being the adult to his child had caused her to shun all vestiges of that sort of behavior when it came to her own living space.

Picking out the largest piece, she brought her plate

with her into the crammed living room. Jaren sank down on the floor, sitting cross-legged in front of the TV. A local news station was on, but her attention was primarily focused on appeasing her growling stomach.

She'd just systematically worked her way through the slice to the end crust when the bell rang. Frowning, she glanced in the door's direction, as if that would be sufficient to make the bell cease trying to claim her attention.

It didn't.

The doorbell rang a second time.

With a sigh, she got up, picked up her plate and walked back to the kitchen. The front door was just off to the side. Setting her plate down on the table, she paused. She hadn't actually made any friends and as far as she knew, no one outside of the Human Resources Department at the precinct even *had* her home address. This had to be a stranger.

For a second, she glanced at her service revolver casually lying on the table beside the pizza box where she'd put it.

Better safe than sorry, she told herself, picking the gun up.

Just then, her cell phone rang. Holding on to her weapon with her right hand, Jaren dug the phone out of her back pocket with her left.

"Hello?"

"Are you planning on opening the door anytime soon, or are you just going to keep staring at it for the rest of the night?"

Startled, Jaren looked around, searching for a hidden

camera. Then, chagrined, she realized that the window over the sink looked out on the space just a few feet shy of her door. Anyone coming up the walk could look in and see her in the kitchen.

Added to that, the voice was familiar. "O'Brien?" she asked even as she told herself she was wrong. They'd just spent the whole day together, basically getting on each other's nerves. There was absolutely no reason for him to be here.

"Good guess," the deep voice on the other end of the cell said. "Now open the damn door."

Still holding her cell phone in her hand, she tucked the service revolver into the back of her jeans and flipped open the lock. She stepped back as she opened the door.

Jaren started to ask if there'd been another vampire slaying and if that was what had brought him to her door when she realized that he was holding something wriggly and caramel-colored in his hands.

All paws and ears, her partner's companion was a puppy—of the mongrel persuasion.

What the hell was O'Brien doing here with a puppy?

Since she was still partially blocking access to her apartment and not saying anything, Kyle asked coolly, "Mind if we come in?"

Jaren cleared her throat and took another step back, clearing a path for him. She was still staring at the extremely animated ball of fluff in his hands. "Who's your friend?"

"She doesn't have a name yet," Kyle told her, struggling to keep the dog close. The puppy seemed just as determined *not* to be kept close. From what she could see of the situation, Jaren mused, O'Brien was the one destined to eventually lose the battle. "I figured you might want to take care of that little detail."

Jaren's eyebrows drew together as she tried to make sense of her partner's answer. "Why would I want to do that?"

"Because she's your dog," he replied simply.

Jaren stared at him. "I don't have a dog."

"You do now," he informed her matter-of-factly. Kyle twisted around, foiling the puppy's attempt to escape by climbing up his shoulder and then diving down to the floor. "My sister's dog, Hussy, had a litter a couple of months ago and she's been trying to find homes for the puppies now that they're weaned."

"Hussy?" she echoed. That seemed like a rather callous name for a pet.

"She gets around," Kyle explained, giving her Greer's reason for selecting the name. "Despite all of Greer's precautions," he added. Greer had given in to the inevitable and was having the dog spayed before she had a chance to beget yet another litter. "Interested?" He seemed to move the puppy toward her as he asked the question.

It was on the tip of Jaren's tongue to politely but firmly refuse the offer. She even got to utter the first few words.

"It's very nice of you to think of me—"

But her refusal got no further. With a little help from Kyle, the puppy took matters into her own paws. Its tongue working faster than a windshield wiper set on High, the puppy began to lick every inch of Jaren's face.

Any resolve Jaren had melted away on the spot. She wasn't even sure just when the transfer was undertaken, when the puppy went from Kyle's hands into hers, but suddenly, there she was, holding on to a wiggling mass of tongue and fur, trying not to laugh as the puppy tickled her earlobe.

But still she valiantly tried to turn away the gift. She had no time for a dog in her life, especially not a puppy. Puppies required care and attention she just didn't have to give—no matter how adorable this one was.

"O'Brien, I can't—"

Kyle didn't let her get any further. "Yes, you can," he insisted. "You'll be doing my sister—and yourself—a favor."

"I don't know your sister and how would this be doing me a favor?"

This was harder than he thought. When he'd stopped by Greer's to pick up the puppy, he'd been fairly certain this was going to be a piece of cake, a win-win situation. Greer would have gotten a good home for one of her puppies, and he wouldn't have to apologize for getting on Rosetti's case. The puppy's very existence would do that for him.

"You said you had a dog that died."

"Yes?" Jaren pressed.

He spelled it out for her. "According to pet owners, once you've been there, once you've had a pet in your life, there's a void that opens up when they're gone that nothing else except another pet can fill."

Okay, he was right, but she had no desire to open

herself up to being hurt again and dogs didn't live nearly long enough.

"I had no idea you had a degree in psychology," she commented wryly.

"Just a student of human nature." A careless shrug accompanied his words.

For her part, Jaren was doing her very best to resist but even she sensed that it was doomed to failure. The puppy was winning her over by the moment.

"In case you haven't noticed, I'm a cop, and as such, I'm out all hours. That wouldn't be fair to the dog. I can't give her the kind of attention she needs and deserves."

Rather than argue, Kyle dug into his back pocket and pulled out a folded, colorful ad. He handed it to her. Jaren opened it and she saw that it was an ad from a local dog walker. The woman had ten dogs of varying size with her and Jaren could have sworn some of them were smiling.

"You have her walk your dog for you, and you'll have a contented and warm friend to come home to. Greer can help you housebreak the dog if you want." Looking around, he broke down. He'd held it back as long as he could. "I thought you said you moved in a couple of weeks ago." It was one of the pieces of information she'd tossed at him during their time together.

"I did."

Two weeks was plenty of time to settle in. It wasn't that big an apartment. "Did the moving van break down?"

What was he getting at—besides her one last nerve? "No, why?"

He peered into the next room. "These things have been here as long as you have?"

"Give or take a day." And then, as he slipped into the next room, it hit her. She thought men felt comfortable around unorganized chaos. Jaren sighed. "You want to know why I haven't unpacked."

"Question did cross my mind." His voice floated in from the second bedroom as Kyle undertook a survey of the rest of the apartment. All the rooms had boxes crowded into them. He thought of his sister and his late mother. "Most women I know are nesters." He walked back into the kitchen. "They like to keep things organized."

"Well, now you know one who doesn't," she told him nonchalantly. "I even hate unpacking groceries," she tagged on.

Kyle peered into the refrigerator, then closed the door. He shook his head. "I guess that would explain it."

*"It?"* she echoed.

His gesture took in the refrigerator and the tiny pantry he'd already looked in. They contained a bottle of water between them. "The lack of foodstuffs."

"Most take-out places cook better than I do," she replied without an iota of self-consciousness.

She would have liked to sound indignant at his prying, but it was hard being indignant about this assault on her housekeeping abilities when her neck was being tickled by a tiny, lightning-fast pink tongue.

Jaren noticed that Kyle was eyeing the pizza.

At least he didn't just help himself, she thought. "Would you like a piece?"

It was all the invitation he needed. He had a weak spot in his heart for pizza.

"Twisted my arm," he declared, flipping open the lid and claiming a large slice for himself. It was only after he'd taken two good-size, healthy bites of the pepperoni-and-sausage concoction that he asked, "So, what's the verdict?" When Jaren looked at him curiously, he nodded toward the puppy that was attempting to scramble up her shoulder. She had a lock of Jaren's blond hair in her mouth.

Using two hands, Jaren drew the puppy back down to chest level. "You mean I have a choice?"

His eyes held hers for a moment. "Everyone's always got a choice."

That was what she'd tried to make her father understand when he'd told her that he just couldn't get himself to quit drinking, that the alcohol just had too strong a hold on him. She'd loved her father dearly, but she'd hated that weak side of him with a passion. The side that hadn't fought to keep her mother in his life, that hadn't fought against the addiction that eventually had destroyed his liver and stolen him from her.

She couldn't think about that now, Jaren silently chided and forced herself to refocus. If there was any doubt in her mind about keeping the dog, it was completely demolished as the puppy all but washed her face with rapid, darting kisses.

Jaren sighed, surrendering. "I guess if it's doing your sister a favor—"

"It would be."

He said it so solemnly, she almost believed him—if it hadn't been for the glint in his eye.

But it was a way not to seem as if she was in his debt, which she knew she was. "Then I guess I'll keep her."

"Good choice." Standing closer to her, he scratched the dog behind her ear. The puppy's panting became audibly loud. "What are you going to name her?"

Jaren held the dog up and away from her for a moment, as if seeing the puppy from a different angle would decide the matter for her.

It did. "Kyle."

Kyle raised an eyebrow as he looked at her, waiting. "Yeah?"

She realized that Kyle thought she was addressing him. Jaren shook her head adamantly. "No, I'm going to name the puppy Kyle."

He'd deliberately picked out the only female in the litter because Jaren had mentioned that her previous dog had been a female. He'd referred to the dog as *she*, but Jaren had obviously missed that.

"That's a guy's name," he pointed out.

Jaren grinned. "Not these days. A lot of names are crossing over. Besides, this way when she chews through my shoes or the bottom of the curtains, I'll think of you."

Kyle shrugged, not entirely displeased at her choice— and that surprised him. "Whatever works for you."

He glanced at his watch. He'd promised his newly acquired cousins, Dax and Clay, that he'd join them and some of the rest of the family for a round of poker tonight at seven at Andrew's house. It was getting close to that time now.

But there was no clock to punch and he knew for a fact other people would be at the table. Hanging around a few more minutes wouldn't matter. No one would miss him for a hand or two.

Wiping his fingers on the back of his jeans, he nodded toward the cardboard towers that were closest to him.

"You want any help with those?"

Jaren looked over her shoulder at the boxes. When she'd packed, she'd just haphazardly thrown everything in without making any discerning choices, telling herself she could do that when she opened the boxes again. But now the day of reckoning was at hand and she didn't feel like facing it.

"You mean like helping me unpack?" she asked, tugging the puppy back down into her arms.

He laughed. "Well, either that, or helping you throw them into the Dumpster."

The second choice was not without appeal. She didn't want to have to deal with memories.

"Don't think I hadn't thought of that," Jaren commented. Shaking her head, she turned down his offer, rather mystified that he actually would offer. There was obviously more to this man than she thought. "No, unpacking is something I'm going to have to get to on my own." She saw the skeptical expression on his face and grasped at the first excuse she could think of. "You wouldn't know where anything went."

"I could ask," he told her pointedly.

He was actually serious, wasn't he? "That's okay. I don't believe in putting guests to work."

"How about friends?" Kyle countered.

She watched him for a long moment, not sure what to make of him or what he'd just said. On the first day they'd worked together, she would have said that he didn't want any part of her.

"You volunteering?" she asked.

He absently petted his namesake. "Makes life easier," he told her.

She laughed softly in disbelief. "Funny, you don't strike me as the warm and toasty type."

"I'm not," he said honestly, then added, "But I've had to make some changes recently." Changes in the way he'd perceived himself, his mother and his siblings. It shook a man to the core to discover that everything he'd believed to be true was actually a lie. "Got me a little ticked off for a while," he admitted, "but I'm starting to handle it."

He'd done it. He'd hooked her. "Do I get to know what *it* is?"

Kyle wasn't the type to share his feelings or private information. That much still remained true despite the changes his life had undergone. Changes that had, at the time, shaken the ground beneath his feet with more force than any magnitude 6.9 earthquake.

But he was still standing and that, he knew, was a good thing. "Maybe when I get to know you better," he qualified.

Curiosity, the intense variety, comprised approximately eighty percent of Jaren's makeup. She *hated* not knowing something. But she was also bright enough to understand that pushing in this case would have the absolute reverse effect.

So, resigned, she nodded in response to his answer and said, "Good enough," even though it wasn't. Shifting the puppy to her other side, she moved toward the door and rested her hand on the knob. "You'd better get going."

Amusement lifted the corners of his mouth. "Throwing me out?"

"More like giving you a way out," she corrected. "You've looked at your watch twice in the last five minutes. That tells me that you have somewhere else you have to be and I don't want to keep you from it."

He hadn't realized that he was being that obvious. "You know, you might just turn out to be a half-decent detective after all."

She laughed briefly. "You're going to wind up a lonely old man if that's an example of the way you flatter a woman."

Opening the front door, Jaren stepped back to let him pass. Kyle, the puppy, burrowed her head against her chest. Jaren smiled. She'd picked the right name after all, she mused.

"Oh, and O'Brien?"

About to cross the threshold out, Kyle turned to look at her. "Yeah?"

"Thanks."

He was completely unprepared for what accompanied the single word of gratitude.

Standing on her toes, Jaren leaned over to brush a quick kiss on his cheek. At least, that had been her intention.

But he'd turned his head too sharply and she'd missed her target.

Her lips brushed against his mouth.

## Chapter 8

Startled, Jaren pulled back as if her lips had come in contact with a hot surface.

She didn't want Kyle to misunderstand and she grabbed onto words to form an apology. But the ones that rose to her lips were never given voice. Something had definitely been triggered—inside of him, as well, if that unguarded look in his eyes was any indication.

So, instead of talking, Jaren found herself leaning into Kyle again.

At the same moment that he leaned into her.

She was surprised and yet, not really. Because, although they were still relative strangers, that *thing* that sizzled between them was older than time. The only one who seemed oblivious was the puppy that Jaren still held in her arms. The dog wiggled, its warm body and whisper-soft fur only adding to the flash and fire that had been inadvertently ignited.

Jaren drew in a deep breath but that in no way managed to stop her head from spinning. It didn't even begin to properly stabilize the room which suddenly tilted.

His mouth was pressed against hers. The kiss was deepening.

Jaren heard herself moan.

Kyle wasn't sure just what he was thinking when he took hold of Jaren's shoulders. Most likely, he'd intended to gently but firmly create a separation between them. But somehow, the gesture was never completed. His hands remained on her shoulders and instead of pushing her back, even a little, he anchored her in place. And struggled against the very real urge to pull her into him. To charge through the door that this unintended kiss had unexpectedly opened.

The impulse was so strong that, for one unsettling moment, Kyle even considered following through. But then the puppy suddenly yelped. The sound drove a wedge between them, returning Kyle to his senses. It apparently did the same for Jaren, he noted, because she pulled back again.

The look in her eyes told him that she felt as unsettled as he did.

Granted, when he'd first met her, he had felt a rather strong attraction to Jaren. That was only natural. She was a knockout. But he had always been able to separate the physical from the emotional, work from his private life.

This moment had blurred the lines rather badly.

Jaren managed to find her tongue—and her wits—before he did. Stepping back into her apartment, one hand holding the puppy as she stroked its soft, furry head with the other, she heard herself murmuring, "Thanks again for the puppy."

It took him a second to realize what she was talking about.

"Don't mention it," he finally answered. Kyle found himself talking to her door. She'd closed it rather quickly at the end of her sentence.

Kyle stood there for a moment, staring at the closed door, his mind a blank for possibly the very first time in his life. And then the question, What the hell had just happened here? echoed in his brain.

No answer came to him.

Shaking off the bewildered feeling, he turned on his heel and walked to the vehicle he'd left standing in guest parking.

Standing a few inches away on the other side of the door, Jaren looked down at the puppy. In the distance, she heard the distinct sound of a car being started up and then pulling away.

O'Brien.

He was leaving.

She let go of the breath she was holding and then drew in another. She released that slowly as she tried to collect herself. Tried to go on with her evening as it had been before everything had been upended.

"Okay, Kyle," she said, addressing the dog, "what was that all about? Do you have a clue?" The puppy began to nibble on her fingertips. "Yeah, me, neither," she admitted with a sigh. "C'mon, let's watch some TV and pretend this never happened. All except for you, of course," she added, leaning her cheek against the top of the puppy's head.

Her heart continued hammering. Hard enough almost to crack her ribs.

When Jaren walked into the squad room the next morning, Kyle wasn't sitting at his desk. Setting down the cardboard tray that held four coffee containers and the box of doughnuts she'd brought in, Jaren looked around the area. No one was around.

It wasn't *that* early, she thought.

Had there been another murder?

No, she decided, someone would have called her.

A moment later, two of the detectives she'd met the other day entered. There was a heavyset man who'd only been introduced to her by his last name—Holloway—and his partner, Diego Sanchez, a ten-year veteran with a quick smile and sharp, brown eyes. Sanchez was half of Holloway's size.

"I brought doughnuts and coffee from the coffee shop down the street," she announced to the two detectives, gesturing toward the offering. "You're both welcome to them."

Holloway, in the process of lowering his girth on to his chair, straightened instantly. For a man his size, he seemed incredibly light on his feet. He crossed from his desk to hers in the blink of an eye.

"Knew I was going to like you the minute I saw you," the detective declared, grinning as he selected a doughnut that was hemorrhaging strawberry jelly.

Jaren returned the smile as she looked around the room. "Have you seen O'Brien around anywhere?" she asked him.

Holloway shook his head, but Sanchez, helping himself to a doughnut with a light dusting of sugar, told her, "He called in this morning and said he had to run an errand first and that he'd be just a little late coming in."

Very little, she thought because, even as Sanchez finished giving her this information, Jaren saw her partner walking into the squad room. He had something tucked under his arm.

"Your partner brought doughnuts," Holloway announced in between appreciative, good-size bites. "How come you never do that?"

"Maybe it's because I don't want to go broke," Kyle answered, deliberately patting Holloway's puddinglike stomach. Opening a drawer on the side of his desk, he dropped whatever he'd brought with him into it and then closed it again.

Holloway pretended to take offense. He did his best to tense his stomach, then patted it. "That's solid muscle, boy."

Kyle laughed. There was nothing solid about it, but he didn't want to point out the fact that Holloway looked like the runner-up in a Santa Claus body-double contest.

"If you say so," Kyle murmured, dropping into his seat.

"I also brought coffee," Jaren said when it was obvious that her partner wasn't going to browse through the large box of doughnuts for a selection. "Asphalt, just the way you like it," she added. She paused to pick up a container that sported a large, red *X* on its white lid. "This one's mine," she told him, removing the lid. The creamy beige surface testified to its composition: one part coffee and two parts pre-sweetened creamer.

Getting up, Kyle glanced at her container and shuddered. "You're welcome to it," he commented. Selecting another container, he removed the lid and looked down at the inky contents. One hearty sip later, he allowed a contented sigh to escape his lips. And then his eyes met hers. "Thanks."

Was it her imagination, or was there an awkwardness shimmering between them? Did he feel it, or was it just her?

Jaren chewed on the inside of her cheek, debating her next move. They were either going to go through the motions of an awkward dance, or move on, placing last night's kiss behind them.

She'd always prided herself on being a direct person. "Look, about last night," she began.

Holloway's desk was a good half room away, but apparently the detective had ears like a bat. He scooted his chair around, *walking* it across the length of the separation until he was all but in her face.

"There was a last night?" he asked with keen interest shining in his small brown eyes.

"There's always a last night," Jaren answered, her voice crisp and detached. "Tonight will be *last night* tomorrow."

Holloway's small eyes narrowed even more. "You've got a college degree, don't you?" he guessed. "In one of those disciplines that don't do you any good, like literature or liberal arts."

She heard the slight note of dismissive disdain. She would have to win her place here. And it wasn't going to be a piece of cake, either. She'd need more than pastries and hot coffee to get into their permanent good graces, Jaren decided. So be it, she was up to it. This wasn't the first time she'd been on the outside, looking for a way in. But she always found one.

She smiled warmly at the big man. "As a matter of fact, my degree's in criminology and I plan on putting it to good use here."

Holloway took the last bite of what was to be just the first part of his breakfast. "Sounds good to me," he told her, selecting another doughnut and then making his way back to his desk.

Jaren picked up a napkin and crossed to the older man's desk. She held it out to him with a smile.

Taking the napkin, Holloway asked, "Where?" She pointed to the corner of his mouth and he wiped away the streak of strawberry jelly that had somehow eluded his consumption.

Kyle observed the interaction with a mixture of amusement and something he couldn't quite identify.

He would have to be careful, he decided. He liked keeping his private life as uncomplicated as possible, and what he'd felt ever so briefly last night was far from uncomplicated. It had all the earmarks of something that could become *very* complicated if he dropped his guard. The shapely lady was trouble. It remained to be seen just how much trouble.

Biding his time, he waited until Jaren looked in his direction. When she did, he shifted his eyes from her face to the door and then back again. The next moment, he got up and crossed to the threshold, walking out.

Jaren waited a couple of minutes before getting up to follow him since that was, she surmised, what he wanted. But just as she pushed her chair back, the phone on her desk rang.

"Rosetti," she announced into the receiver.

"Detective, this is Dr. Carter. The M.E.," the raspy voice on the other end of the line added when she made no response. "You and O'Brien want to come down to the morgue for that autopsy on the latest guy to get a stake through his heart, or do you just want me to send it up when it's typed?"

She tried to think like O'Brien. In his shoes, she would have wanted the autopsy five minutes ago. Preferably written. But in this case, a verbal one was going to have to do.

"We'll come down," she said.

But even as the words came out of her mouth, she couldn't help wondering if O'Brien was going to be bent out of shape that she made the decision for them. After all, any way you looked at it, O'Brien was the senior detective on this and she didn't want him to think she was trying to usurp him, especially after last night. Some men would see what happened as calculated on her part, trying to exercise control over the man by means of sex. The only thing was, that spontaneous combustion reaction between them had caught her by surprise just as much as it had him.

Jaren hurried into the hallway, only to find Kyle leaning against the wall closest to the door. He was obviously waiting for her.

But before he could say anything, she started talking. "The M.E. just called. He wants to see us at the morgue. He said he just completed the autopsy on the Count and thought you might be interested in getting the verbal report."

Kyle wondered if there was something unusual about it—other than the cause of death. Most likely, it was just Carter's way of getting a little attention. Being a medical examiner seemed like a lonely choice of a career, considering all the choices the man could have made with a medical degree. But he'd heard that Wayne Carter wasn't much of a people person and *patients* who couldn't answer back suited him just fine.

"Morgue it is," Kyle agreed, straightening. He took the lead, heading for the elevators.

Jaren fell into step beside him. Kyle still hadn't said anything when they reached the elevators. "Did you want to say something to me?"

Pressing the down button, he glanced at her. "Like what?"

"I don't know. In the squad room, you looked at me

and then indicated the door so when you got up and walked out, I thought you wanted me to follow you."

Kyle debated yanking her chain a little more—after all, she was the one responsible for his sleepless night—then decided there was nothing to be gained by playing games. He was ordinarily above that. He shrugged now, as if what he'd intended on telling Jaren really wasn't all that important.

"I was just going to warn you about Holloway and Sanchez. They like getting on the new kid's case. Right now, that happens to be you." They arrived in the basement and the doors opened for them. "But you seem to be holding your own."

She stepped out before Kyle, then turned to look at him. "Thanks."

He brushed off her gratitude. "Still, if I were you, I wouldn't give them any loaded lines, at least not for a while."

The smile that curved the corners of her mouth was rueful. "You mean like *about last night.*"

He struggled to suppress the smile that automatically came to his lips as the memory of the unsettling kiss feathered through his brain. "That phrase does come to mind."

"Okay, since we're alone," she began, lowering her voice. "About last night—" Jaren took a breath. Kyle said nothing as he went on watching her. Jaren moistened her lips. With just a little imagination, she could still taste him. "I don't want you to think that I—"

She was squirming, he thought. Initially, he'd expected that this might amuse him a little, but it didn't. He didn't want her to feel uncomfortable, not about that. He didn't want to hear her make any protests about the kiss that had caught them both by surprise. Some things were better left alone and unexplored.

"I don't," he told her briskly, cutting Jaren off.

Jaren stared at him. She opened her mouth to ask Kyle just exactly what he thought she was going to say, then decided that maybe, in this case, it was better to let sleeping dogs lie. Besides, it would never happen again. She didn't believe in getting involved with coworkers.

"Okay. By the way, why were you late?" she asked, putting the sensitive topic to rest.

He started walking. Since she had no idea where the morgue was, Jaren fell in just a half step behind him, letting him lead the way.

"I went to the evidence room and checked out one of the copies of the book we found at the first two murders. It was the neurosurgeon's copy," he added before she could ask—not that it made any difference whose copy he had. Both were pristine, with no markings on the pages.

Jaren looked at him in surprise. "You mean *The Vampire Diaries?*"

He couldn't help the condescending frown that rose to his lips. He still didn't understand how anyone would want to read that kind of drivel. For that matter, he couldn't see how a publishing company would want to place their logo on the spine of something so demeaning.

"That's the one."

"I could have given you my copy last night."

"It didn't occur to me last night," he told her honestly.

"Why did it occur to you this morning?" Jaren asked.

He continued leading the way down the winding hallway. Jaren looked around, trying to take note of the numbers on the closed doors they passed. Right about now, she regretted not bringing bread crumbs with her to mark her path.

He shrugged casually. "Thought it might help me get into the killer's mind."

Score one for her side, Jaren thought. "So you *do* think the book has something to do with the murders," she said.

"I haven't made up my mind about that, but it can't hurt to get familiar with the work, just in case it *is* tied into the murders."

Even as he said it, it still sounded utterly ridiculous to his ear. Someone was slaying vampires, or people that he or she *believed* to be vampires. It sounded like a bad plot hastily thrown together for some movie-of-the-week program on one of the lesser cable channels.

Kyle looked at Jaren just before he pushed open the door and walked into the morgue. "I like covering all my bases."

Jaren surprised him by nodding. Her expression was completely serious. "So do I."

# *Chapter 9*

Jaren expected the morgue in Aurora to be similar to the one she'd been to in Oakland: an eerily quiet place where the attendants moved around like wraiths on rubber-soled shoes. If they spoke at all, they kept their voices at a low level out of respect for the dead. Should music be part of the scene, something classical or very low-keyed would be piped in.

What she definitely did *not* expect was to walk into the middle of a rousing John Philip Sousa march.

Startled by the blaring rendition, Jaren halted right before the door and looked at Kyle. "Are we in the right place?"

Pushing the door open, Kyle gestured toward the wall comprised of closed, large metal drawers, behind which rested the latest group of homicide victims and deceased people whose manner of death raised questions.

"It's the morgue all right," he told her. Kyle raised his voice to be heard above the crash of cymbals. "The M.E. likes to counterbalance the solemnity of death with a little cheery music."

"There's cheery and then there's deafening," she pointed out.

This was downright weird, she thought. But not at all creepy. Looking around, Jaren saw the man who had summoned them a few minutes ago.

There was no one else in the room—if you didn't count the body he was presently working on.

Rail-thin, Dr. Wayne Carter seemed taller than he actually was. A welcoming smile curved his mouth when he glanced up and saw them entering the morgue. He waited until they'd both crossed to him.

"You must be the new homicide detective," he said to Jaren.

Her smile felt tight and forced. So-called cheerful music or not, this was definitely not her favorite place. "I must be."

"You'll forgive me if I don't shake hands," Carter said, nodding at her and then at the man standing beside her.

Jaren looked at the M.E.'s rubber gloves. They, as well as his blue paper smock, were covered with blood. He'd obviously just concluded the autopsy right before he'd called them.

"More than forgive you," she assured him.

Kyle got down to the reason they were there. "What's wrong with this one, Doc?"

Carter eyed the ragged clothes and black cape neatly folded on the counter behind him. Until several hours ago, they had been all but hermetically sealed to the vagrant known as the Count.

"In this case, it would be easier to say what wasn't wrong," Carter responded.

Kyle was amenable to playing along—up to a point. "I'll bite. What *wasn't* wrong?"

Carter's voice grew more expansive, as if he was conducting a lecture in a classroom. He milked the moment.

"Given the kind of life the Count had to have led on the street, his liver is in remarkable condition." He looked at Jaren, addressing the words to her as if he were in charge of her personal edification. "Most people on the street tend to have livers that are on the way out, thanks to incredible alcohol abuse."

Expecting some sort of litany, Kyle waited for more. There wasn't any. "That's it?"

The M.E. spread his hands. "That's it."

"Cause of death?" Kyle pressed. Carter raised his eyes from the body he had just now finished sewing up again and gave him an incredulous look. "I have to ask," Kyle explained.

"A wooden stake driven through his heart," Carter replied and then he paused, as if debating whether or not to ask the next question. "Is there *really* some nut out there running around and trying to make the world safe from vampires?"

The question was for both the detectives in the room, but Carter ended it by shifting his quizzical eyes toward Jaren.

It was Kyle who answered. "It's shaping up that way," he conceded reluctantly. The idea still didn't sit right with him. He felt he was being deliberately played.

Jaren, he noted, looked preoccupied. The next moment, she moved over to the dispenser on the wall and pulled out two rubber gloves. Slipping them on, she picked up the dark, wooden stake that the M.E. had placed on the counter next to the current victim's clothing. She examined the stake carefully, then addressed the M.E.

"What kind of wood is this?" she asked Carter.

The M.E. nodded. "O'Brien said you'd want to know so I had the guys at CSI run it for you." He paused, as if waiting for some kind of a drumroll. He had to settle for another crash of cymbals instead. "That is Brazilian hardwood," he told her, raising his voice again. "It's pretty rare around here."

Jaren turned the stake over in her hand. Did that have some kind of significance, or had it just been handy for some reason when the killer had murdered the neurosurgeon?

Looking up at the M.E. she asked, "Are you saying that someone went all the way down to Brazil to carve the stakes?"

Thin shoulders moved vaguely up and down beneath the blue paper gown. Carter pulled it off and deposited the cover into a nearby wastepaper basket. "I'm saying that your killer is a very organized, didactic person, maybe even superstitious." He regarded the table at the latest victim. "This has all the earmarks of a ritual slaying."

Jaren tried to make sense out of what Carter was saying. "So, you think he stalked them and then killed them?"

"Sounds like a theory," Kyle allowed noncommittally. He heard the doubt in her voice. "Why, what's your take on it?"

She didn't have a definite take on it. She felt like someone stumbling around in the dark, knowing that there was a light switch somewhere. If she only could find it.

"Maybe he's just prepared," she guessed, thinking out loud. "He has the stakes in his car just in case he comes up against another *vampire*." And then an idea hit her. "Maybe he's just a slayer, not a hunter." She saw the skepticism in Kyle's eyes. Not that she blamed him. "Protecting himself preemptively rather than just looking for a fight."

Kyle wasn't sure where she was going with this. "So, we do what, get on TV and tell everyone who bought that stupid book to get rid of it? And not to wear any clothes that might be mistakenly identified as something a vampire might wear?"

"Does sound pretty stupid when you say it out loud like that," she agreed. "Although we are dealing with someone who's a few cards shy of a full deck."

"Or wants us to think that he or she is," Kyle countered.

So many ways to go with this, Jaren thought, frustrated. Just exploring the options made her tired. She looked down again at the stake in her hand. Was this a clue, or a red herring? Most of the time, killers were just ordinary people trying to get away with their crimes. But once in a while, they turned out to be far more diabolical than anything found in a novel. Which one was this?

"So, if I wanted more of these hardwood stakes," she said, turning back to the M.E., "I'd do what, go off to Brazil?"

Carter thought for a moment. "Or check with some of the exclusive landscapers and nurseries. See if anyone recently either purchased a Brazilian hardwood tree—"

"Or had one cut down and ground up," Kyle interjected.

Was he humoring her, or was he serious? She still had trouble reading Kyle's expression. "Sounds a little out there," she admitted.

They were past the point of *a little out there.* It was more like *a lot out there.*

"So is driving a stake through someone's heart," Kyle answered. He turned to Carter. "So, how soon can I have the official report?"

"All in due time, O'Brien, all in due time." Carter stripped off the gloves he'd used for the autopsy and threw them into the trash after his paper gown. "By the way, who do I release the first victim to?" he asked. "I'm all done with the autopsy and I sent the report over yesterday." He waved a hand around the area. "I've got a storage crunch going on."

"Who asked for the body?", Kyle asked.

"That's just it," Carter told him. "Nobody requested the remains."

"Nobody?" Jaren echoed. This was a man who interacted with a great many people every day. He wasn't some hermit found by the wayside like the Count. "But he was married."

"Divorced," Carter corrected. He picked up the file he'd comprised from his desk and waved it for emphasis. "And I tried calling his ex, but she said she didn't care if I turned the good doctor into fertilizer and sprinkled him around in some park—preferably an out-of-state one." Carter opened the folder and glanced down a page to check his facts. "His receptionist told me that there was no next of kin, no parents, no kids and she has no idea if the man had any siblings." Closing the folder, he dropped it back on his desk. "He never mentioned any, and there were no burial instructions."

"That's because he thought he was immortal," Jaren surmised quietly, voicing the thought more to herself. She looked over toward the wall of drawers. "Which drawer is his?"

After removing the face mask that still dangled about his neck, Carter tossed it onto the counter and crossed over to the extreme left of the room where the drawers were. They housed the bodies either waiting for an autopsy or a ride to the funeral parlor.

He pulled open the bottom one.

Following him, Jaren gazed down at the surgeon's lifeless face. The vampire slayer's first known victim was already turning blue.

From everything they'd learned about the surgeon, he was insufferable, if exceedingly talented. A lot of people were probably glad he was out of their lives. But somehow, having him lying here, unclaimed like a forgotten lump of clay just didn't seem right. At least, it didn't sit right with her.

"What do you do with bodies that no one claims?" she asked Carter.

But it was Kyle who answered her. Intrigued by the expression on her face, he moved a little closer to her. "The city comes up with a little cash to bury them in Potter's Field."

She shook her head. "Not right," he thought he heard her whisper. "It's just not right." It wasn't as if the surgeon lacked for money. He just had no one who cared. Impulsively, she turned toward Carter and said, "If no one turns up to make arrangements for him, let me know."

Kyle exchanged glances with the M.E. "If you don't mind my asking," he inquired of Jaren, "why?"

"Because if no one else comes forward, I'll make the arrangements for the funeral," she told him.

"But you don't know this guy from Adam," Kyle pointed out. "I mean, other than the fact that we caught this homicide, you have no connection to him. Do you?"

"No," she told him firmly. "But it's just sad that no one cares enough about him to step forward." She turned to face her partner and noticed that both he and the M.E. were watching her as if they thought she'd lost her mind. But dealing with her father had shown her that there were always two sides to everything, if not more. "What does that say about the sum total of the man's life?"

"That he reaped what he sowed?" Kyle put in archly.

"Maybe so, but it still doesn't make it right."

Kyle had another guess for her. "How about *what goes around, comes around?*"

This time, Jaren smiled. "I'm counting on it."

Kyle didn't understand immediately, and then her meaning dawned on him. "You're hoping that when your time comes, that—"

Jaren waved away the rest of his words, not wanting to hear them. Somehow, hearing the sentiment spoken made her sound calculating, and she'd never been that.

"Yeah, yeah, yeah, okay, you've proven your point. You're good at guessing and piecing things together," she granted him. Turning toward Carter, she said, "Don't forget, call me if no one turns up to take care of our neurosurgeon."

"You're almost as good as called," Carter told her as she walked out.

Jaren walked slightly ahead of Kyle on the way back to the elevators. One arrived almost as soon as she pushed the up button. Stepping in, she was keenly aware that her partner studied her. The fact that he wasn't saying anything just seemed to make it worse.

She pushed the button for their floor.

"What?" she finally asked, unable to figure out if she'd said the wrong thing, or if something else was on Kyle's mind. Was he thinking about last night? Because she was, no matter how much she tried to shut it out of her mind.

The shrug was vague and dismissive. "Just trying to figure you out, Rosetti."

"Do yourself a favor and don't," she suggested, echoing the same sentiment he'd expressed on their first day together. "Just enjoy the ride," she instructed glibly.

The lazy smile that whispered over his lips told her that Kyle was already doing that.

"Okay, now what?" she asked.

The elevator doors opened and they walked toward their squad room. "You up for some more canvasing?" he asked.

"More than up for it," she told him.

Being downstairs in the morgue made her feel restless and unsettled. She didn't think she could concentrate if confined behind her desk right now. At least out on the street, she had an excuse to move around.

Grabbing her jacket from the back of her chair, Jaren said, "Lead the way."

They went back to the scene of the latest slaying. Jaren was both surprised and pleased to see that the area where the Count had been killed was now commemorated with a small collection of prayer candles of varying sizes and colors. Their flames flickered in the afternoon breeze like so many minions paying their last respects.

"I guess people really did like him," she commented to her partner.

Maybe if they'd shown the man this kind of attention when he'd been alive, he might have been able to turn his life around, she thought. But then, according to what she'd heard from the handful of people she managed to interview last night, the Count was content with the life he'd chosen for himself.

Maybe he actually was happy.

Kyle's next words confirmed her suspicions. "He was a character, part of the decor. I think a lot of people tried to help him over the years, but he wouldn't have any of it." Bending over, Kyle picked up a card that had fallen over and righted it. "He liked being the eccentric figure, leaning on his staff and spinning lies, reciting them as if they were pure gospel."

"Anyone else like him around?" Back in Oakland, all they'd had were the usual collection of homeless people. No one stood out the way the Count had.

"Not to my knowledge, but then the Count left a void. Somebody'll be along to fill it soon enough," Kyle speculated. "Why, think that'll be the next victim?"

"You never know," she replied, then shrugged. "Just trying to stay one step ahead of the killer."

He laughed a little. So far, three murders and they hadn't been able to catch a break. "And how's that working for you?"

"It's not," she admitted ruefully. Standing beside the restaurant Dumpster, Jaren scanned the area. There was an apartment building not far off whose back windows looked down into the alley.

Eight stories, she counted. And a lot of windows. That made potentially a great many people to interview.

"How do you want to do this?" she asked him.

He was already walking out of the alley. The building's entrance was on the opposite side. "We'll go floor by floor."

We. As in together. "I thought you might want to divide up the apartments." She was irked he didn't suggest it but made her feel as if she needed supervision. "I'm not a rookie, you know."

"I know," he answered mildly. He could sense her agitation. He just wanted to observe her a little more.

Strictly for work purposes, he silently added, then grew annoyed with himself for feeling that was even necessary. "Maybe I believe that two heads are better than one."

And if she believed that, he had a bridge he wanted to sell her, she thought. He didn't trust her yet, but that was okay. She was patient, she could wait him out.

Besides, she was accustomed to having to prove herself. There had been a few tough sells on the force in Oakland, but by the time she left, they had all been won over. And—she slanted a glance at her partner— she intended to do the same thing here.

Eventually, O'Brien was going to have to admit that she did more than just a decent job. God knew she was ready to run with the ball—if only he'd give it to her.

Until he did, she would go along and play his game. Nothing would be gained by crossing him or going behind his back. Those were plays she had reserved for desperate times, when her gut told her she could succeed and there was no other way left to go.


The canvas yielded nothing.

Almost no one looked out their window the night the

Count had died, not even out of boredom. The one man who had gone to the window when he thought he *heard a strange noise* hadn't seen anything. Fortunately for the killer and unfortunately for them, it had been a moonless night.

They kept at it for hours, until they'd interviewed every one of the tenants who were home.

"That went well," Jaren said sarcastically as they left the pre-1960s building. "What's next, fearless leader?"

He led the way back to his car. He'd left the vehicle parked by the curb. Two other cars had pulled in, one in front, one behind. Between them they'd left half an inch of space. This was going to take maneuvering, he thought, annoyed.

"Next you start calling landscapers and nurseries to see if anyone ordered or cared for a Brazilian hardwood tree in the last five years."

She didn't bother to ask why he'd given her the assignment. She knew. "My idea."

"Your idea," he answered. "Start with the phonebook and work your way to the Internet."

"Why don't I do it the other way around? Might save some time," she suggested. "Everyone advertises on the Internet these days."

"Not if they want my business," he commented.

"You don't like the Internet." The remark was accompanied by an amused smile.

"It's an annoying invasion of privacy," he said dismissively.

"It's also a hell of a fast way to locate things."

The look on Kyle's face told her he far preferred the old-fashioned way of information gathering—applying shoe leather to the pavement.

Jaren smiled to herself. It was nice to know that her partner had flaws.

# Chapter 10

"You look dead on your feet," Kyle commented the next morning as he came in and sat down at his desk.

He'd deliberately come in early to get a jump start on things and was surprised to see that Jaren was there ahead of him. Unlike the previous time, she'd changed her clothing so she obviously had gone home the night before. Since their desks butted up against one another, he had an unobstructed view of her face. While disconcertingly attractive, she definitely looked like a woman in desperate need of a nap.

Kyle cocked his head and peered at her face now. "You get any sleep last night?"

The truth was that she'd only beaten him here by about ten minutes. She'd come in early because she was afraid she'd oversleep if she stayed in bed that so-called extra five minutes. Ringing alarms had no effect on her when she was sleeping. One of the few comments she could remember her mother making was that she could probably sleep through a grade 8 earthquake.

Jaren shrugged in response to his question. Picking up her mug of coffee, she held it in both hands and took a long sip before answering. "Some."

"Puppy keeping you up?" Kyle guessed.

"Indirectly," she allowed. Taking another hit of almost black coffee—hating the taste but thinking it would help make her come around—she elaborated. "I came home to find that she had chewed the corners on most of the boxes in the living room and bedroom."

Jaren's mouth curved in a small, fond smile. No doubt about it. It was love at first sight between her and the puppy. She supposed that she owed O'Brien for that.

"I think that was her subtle way of telling me to unpack, so I did. I hate stopping anything in the middle," she admitted, "so I was unpacking until one this morning." Leaning back in her chair, Jaren sighed and shook her head as if she couldn't quite believe it. "I didn't realize that I had so much stuff until I had to try to find a place for it all in the apartment."

He'd never had that kind of problem. Unlike Greer, he'd always been a minimalist. "Maybe you need a larger apartment."

Jaren's eyes widened and she appeared completely awake for the first time since he'd walked in.

"You mean move? Uh-uh, this is it," she swore vehemently. "I'm staying in this place until I die. No more packing and unpacking for me."

This had been her first experience with moving. In Oakland, she'd continued to live with her father even after she'd hit the age when most people moved out of their childhood homes. Afflicted with a failing liver and kidneys, her father had needed care. Jaren had seen no point in trying to maintain two separate households.

"I'm not going anywhere until someone finds a way to transport my apartment from one location to another—intact—without me having to do anything," Jaren added with feeling.

He laughed, amused because she sounded so serious. "You finished moving in, then?"

"Not yet," she confessed. "But almost."

There were still a few more boxes in the spare bedroom, but she'd been too exhausted to open them. Those she planned to get to tonight—if her puppy didn't beat her to it and chew her way through them.

Kyle debated volunteering his sister's help. Greer was a whiz at organizing things and she liked nothing better than doing just that. His thought was interrupted when he saw the lieutenant walking out of his small office.

Barone came directly to Kyle's desk.

The man wasted no words. "The Chief of Ds wants us to put a task force together before the city starts to panic that there's some kind of vampire-slaying weirdo out there."

"So now, instead of two of us being up against a dead end, we'll have company?" Kyle asked archly.

The lieutenant frowned. "That *dead end* had better crumple soon," he warned. "You know what happens when the public feels their police department isn't looking out for them—they start taking the law into their own hands." That was the last thing any of them wanted. And then he got back to business. He glanced at the notation he'd made while on the phone with Brian Cavanaugh. "Okay, you've got Holloway and Sanchez, plus McIntyre and Chang."

"Which McIntyre?" Kyle asked.

The lieutenant's expression indicated that he had assumed Kyle knew which one before the call came in. "You're related to them now, don't you guys talk?" he asked.

"Haven't seen any of them lately," Kyle admitted grudgingly.

Jaren had the impression that the last time he interacted with any of his new extended family was when he'd taken her to dinner. She simply didn't understand that. If she were part of a large family like that, she'd find opportunities to hang out with them.

"I think it's Riley," the lieutenant answered. "And, if that's not enough, the Chief of Ds said the money to bring in more detectives will be found. He wants results. As in yesterday," Barone emphasized. He gestured beyond the squad room. "You can use the conference room to get organized," he added, then looked from Kyle to Jaren. "Any questions?"

"None that I can think of," Kyle said.

The lieutenant nodded. "Keep me in the loop. I want

daily updates," he said, obviously anticipating that he would be quizzed daily about the progress himself. With that, he walked back into his office.

"And the fun and games continue," Kyle murmured under his breath. "C'mon," he urged Jaren as he rose to his feet. "Let's go get set up in the conference room."

Holloway and Sanchez had just come in, the former juggling a take-out breakfast housed within a large foam container.

"You two are with us," Kyle said, walking past them. "Lieutenant's orders."

"We get to work the vampire slayings?" Holloway asked.

"You get to work the vampire slayings," Kyle affirmed, leading the way out and down the hall to the conference room.

The conference room appeared relatively cheery, thanks to the invasion of the morning sun. It contained just a conference table with its accompanying chairs and a single white bulletin board, a holdover from the last time a task force had made use of the room. At the moment, the board was empty except for the handful of colorful magnets that were clustered in the upper right hand corner.

Hopefully, it wouldn't be filled up, Jaren thought. As far as they knew, there were only three victims.

*Only* she silently mocked herself. Since when had that word become part of the equation? Even one life so callously lost was too many.

Behind her, several technicians entered, some push-

ing carts with landlines, others bringing in slim comput-
ers to hook up and get running.

This was taking on all the characteristics of a major
operation. Even though it was her first of this propor-
tion, Jaren prayed it would be closed down soon and that
the case would wrap up.

Opening up the folder she'd thought to bring with
her, Jaren took out the three eight-by-ten photographs
of the victims as they had appeared in life, before
they'd met the business end of a wooden stake. She'd
gotten the Count's from the human-interest newspaper article that had been written about him a couple
of years ago.

She placed the photographs at the top of the board
in chronological order, then carefully wrote in their
names with a red marker just below the border of each
photograph.

Behind her, she heard one technician begin to open
up the tip lines. It was only a matter of time before they
were inundated with *helpful* information. Crazies would
start phoning in, people who lived humdrum lives and
tried to infuse them with a little drama by convincing
themselves that they had caught a glimpse of the vampire slayer. She wasn't looking forward to that.

But she knew that if they were patient enough,
somewhere amid the hundreds and hundreds of calls
destined to come in, someone just might have a genuine sighting.

That's all they needed, just one legitimate tip. One
thing to get them on their way to tracking down the

killer. In the interim, they would continue sifting through the information they had, trying to gather more and somehow make sense of it.

Once the other two detectives who were assigned to the task force arrived, Kyle addressed the group, handing out assignments and urging follow-ups to the calls they'd already gotten via regular channels. Everything had to be checked out and nothing—no matter how off-the-wall, trivial or preposterous—could be dismissed. Time and again, they'd discovered that truth was stranger than fiction.

When he finished, Kyle turned toward Jaren. "You get anywhere with those landscapers?"

She shook her head. "Not so far. Everyone I've contacted hasn't done any landscaping with a Brazilian hardwood tree. Some of them didn't even know what I was talking about," she added.

But even as Jaren volunteered the information, she knew that she could have been lied to. If she'd spoken to someone who actually knew something, they might have elected to remain silent for their own reasons. A lot of police work boiled down to simple luck. Luck that the killer would slip up, luck that they would stumble onto a clue. Luck that, if she actually found the killer, he could be captured without taking out one of them.

Despite the fact that she had been the one who advanced the theory in the first place, Jaren wasn't a hundred percent convinced that the killer actually saw himself with a mission to slay vampires. It could, after all, just be a clever cover. The killer might want to create a general panic and hide the one—or two—murders behind an incredible smoke screen so that his true intent was not discovered.

How could she decide which was the truth?

Jaren looked at Kyle and sighed. "There are just too many possibilities here, too many forks in the road that might or might not have been taken." She supposed she could draw up a flowchart, playing out the various different scenarios. Maybe seeing it in front of her would help her decide which theory to advance.

"That's why they pay us the big bucks," Riley McIntyre quipped as she walked into the squad room, bringing in her own giant container of coffee. "To sift through all the information and come up with some kind of conclusion." She grinned at Jaren. "Nice to be working with you." She looked around at the other detectives. "For once, I won't feel so outnumbered here."

"Playtime is later, ladies," Kyle informed them. He gestured over toward the bulletin board. "Right now, we've got work to do."

"That's why we're here," Riley answered, a bright, wide smile on her lips.

After two weeks, Jaren felt like she'd been working the vampire-slayer case forever.

Without any tangible result.

Although she liked to think that she was patient, the lack of headway was definitely getting to Jaren. Every call that had been received on their *tip* line was dutifully logged in and investigated. Because of the nature of the murders, she had spoken to a number of men and women whose souls, she was firmly convinced, had been sold or had gone missing in action. People who unwaveringly believed that they had a true connection to the dark side. Detective or not, it was hard for her to reconcile herself to the fact that these people existed.

And then there was the matter of the book. Instead of a drop due to fear, sales of *The Vampire Diaries* had gone through the roof.

"Why?" she murmured to herself under her breath as she read the latest sale figures on the Internet.

"Why what?" Kyle asked, hearing her mutter the question as he walked by her desk.

She raised her eyes to look at him, then waved her hand at her monitor in disgust. "That book we found at the scene of the first two murders, *The Vampire Diaries.* We still don't know what connection, if any, the book had to the actual murders. Maybe it even triggered the attacks, we don't know. You'd think that people would avoid having it in their possession, just in case. Instead, the bookstores can't keep that damn book in stock. It's literally flying off the shelves. What the hell is the matter with people? They're all acting like it's the forbidden fruit and they all want a bite."

Except when it came to his job, Kyle had long since given up trying to understand the workings of the average mind. He shrugged now.

"They want to live dangerously," he concluded. "For most of them, this is the closest they'll come to walking on the wild side and they all crave that thrill of danger, that rush that comes with a vicarious ride—because at the bottom they're certain it *is* a vicarious ride. Why do people go to slasher movies geared to scare them?" he posed. "Same reason. They want to experience that adrenaline rush without really endangering themselves."

She supposed that made as much sense as anything. "You still have the copy you got out of evidence?" she asked.

He shook his head. Looking the book over had proved to be a waste of time. "No, I logged it back in."

The book was over four hundred pages long. "You're that fast a reader?"

He laughed. He tended to skim, but he'd never managed to become one of those speed readers who absorbed everything.

"It wasn't so much a matter of being fast as it was of being bored." In his opinion, it was all purple prose, overdone and badly written. "I still don't understand how that kind of drivel gets published—or manages to gain a legitimate audience. If it wasn't for these murders giving it publicity, I'm sure the sales would have been abysmal." And then he recalled that she had a copy. "What made you buy it?"

"I didn't," she informed him. "Someone back in Oakland gave it to me as a going-away gift." The book had come from Delia, the chief's administrative assistant, a flighty woman who meant well but was far from being a student of human nature. "Someone who obviously didn't know me well enough to know what holds my interest."

Kyle grinned. "So, you don't find it exciting to have a lover who likes to sink his teeth into your neck and can sprout wings at the first sign of dusk?"

She watched him for a long moment. "In my experience, lovers don't need to see the first signs of dusk to take flight so much as hear the word *commitment*. In their language, they hear the word *trapped* and they can't wait to put distance between themselves and the object of their former affection."

There was a significant enough amount of passion behind her words for Kyle to make the logical conclusion. "Someone take off on you, Rosetti?"

She raised her chin and in so doing, dropped a curtain down between them. Her frustration had made her sloppy, she told herself. "I was thinking about a couple of my girlfriends."

He watched her expression, not fully buying into her explanation. "But not you."

"But not me," she affirmed with feeling. While friendly, she still didn't believe in allowing people into her private life until she trusted them. She didn't know O'Brien well enough. "I'm too busy to lay any foundations for a relationship that would frighten off a lover," she told him matter-of-factly.

It wasn't often that his curiosity was aroused when it came to something other than a case. But Rosetti had succeeded in making him curious. "Recently, or always?" he asked.

"Are you interrogating me, O'Brien?"

A careless shrug prefaced his answer. "Nope. Just

taking time to get to know the new kid," he told her with sufficient disinterest.

They'd all been putting in extra time, trying to solve the case before another victim turned up with a piece of wood driven through his chest. Every spare piece of energy was dedicated to finding the killer. Why was O'Brien suddenly wasting time with personal questions? And why, given her friendly nature, did that make her squirm inside? "And just how's *getting to know* me going to help solve this case?"

"It won't solve the case," he told her seriously, his voice low. "But it's good to know a little about the person who's supposed to have your back."

He had her there. She could understand the validity of his reasoning. But, since he opened the door, she had a question of her own, one that had been knocking around the back chambers of her mind.

"Okay, I'll buy that," she granted. He was about to get up when she stopped him with her question. "Why did you bring me a puppy?"

The question had come out of nowhere. He thought they'd already settled that the evening he gave her the puppy.

Kyle sank back down in his seat. "Excuse me?"

"Kyle. The retriever," Jaren specified, in case he thought she was referring to him by his first name. Lately, she only did that in the privacy of her own mind, where she could get intimate without consequence. "Why did you bring her to me that night?"

The expression on his face was meant to tell her that

what he'd done was no big deal, just a matter of logic, nothing more. "I told you, my sister was trying to find homes for her dog's puppies."

No, he'd gone out of his way to get her address and to be deliberately kind to her. This, after making her feel like an outsider. She just wanted to understand which the real Kyle O'Brien was. "I couldn't have been the only dogless person you knew."

He rose again, signaling the conversation was over. "You'd be surprised."

It wasn't over for her. "You always avoid answering questions this way?"

"No. Sometimes I don't say anything at all." He paused. He hadn't meant to sound so curt, but lack of sleep was getting to him, as well. "Okay, you want to know why I brought over the puppy? You looked like you needed a friend and I figured that I'd been kind of rough on you that day. It just seemed like a good match at the time." He had a feeling that Rosetti was the type who never let up so he diverted the conversation away from his motives. "Speaking of which, how's it going?"

"You were right," she admitted, allowing a fond smile to surface. The smile was actually meant for the puppy they were discussing. "It was a good match. She's really smart and she learns fast."

"Must be the name," he commented.

She didn't bother suppressing the grin that came to her lips. "Must be."

"C'mon," he urged. "Let's hit the pavement. I want to reinterview a couple of the neurosurgeon's former patients. Since there haven't been any more *slayings*, I'm thinking that maybe the idea that one murder was planned and the others done as a cover-up might not be that far-fetched."

Jaren was on her feet before he finished his statement.

*They're coming!*

Sweating profusely, he bolted upright in bed. His heart was pounding so hard, it almost exploded out of his chest.

That was Derek's voice, calling to him. Warning him. Derek always knew where the danger was.

There were lights everywhere, but still his eyes darted around, searching the corners of his vast bedroom. Safe, he wanted to be safe.

When was he ever going to be safe?

Despite all the crosses he had hung about the room and the large gold one he wore around his neck—a gift from his protector, "To keep you safe when I can't," he'd told him—he was still afraid.

Afraid because he'd heard the warning. Derek's warning that they were regrouping.

And coming for him.

Unless he got them first.

Hands shaking, he threw off the covers and got out of bed. He was fully clothed. He never undressed anymore. Not since the Protector had been taken from him. He had to be ready to flee into the night if it came to that.

He knew he had to destroy the next one. The one that was out there, waiting for him. After the last, he'd thought, hoped, *prayed* that he was finally safe.

But he wasn't, he thought, angry tears gathering in his eyes. He was never going to be safe. Not until every one of them was dead.

Such a monumental task, and he was only one lone warrior. But it had to be done. He knew the consequences if it wasn't.

For a second, he closed his eyes, praying. Seeking strength in his holy battle against the undead. The words the Protector had taught came back to him. They, and the cross he wore—he told himself, his fingers curling around it now—would keep him safe. And someway, somehow, he was going to kill them all. And only then would he have everlasting peace.

He went to arm himself.

# Chapter 11

It was another long, tiring, fruitless day.

Kyle and Jaren had reinterviewed several people but their efforts yielded no more information. For the most part, they all had the same thing to say about the slain neurosurgeon. Dr. Barrett was an excellent surgeon, with few equals, but no one had wanted to share even an elevator ride with him. He had made no attempt to hide his God complex.

"I don't see wanting to kill someone because he was cold and detached," Jaren commented as they walked away from their last interview—Dr. James Wiley, an orthopedic surgeon Dr. Barrett had treated a year ago. Dr. Wiley had made time for them during his weekly golf game.

"And yet, someone killed him," Kyle countered as they walked to his vehicle.

"Maybe Dr. Barrett was one of the camouflage murders," she suggested. "If we're working with that theory," she added, glancing toward Kyle.

"For lack of anything better." Fantastic as it seemed, he kept coming back to the vampire-slayer theory. *Her* initial theory. Kyle felt he might need a vacation. "I don't know about you, but my brain is beginning to hurt."

"I'm getting a headache," she admitted. "How many more of the doctor's patients do you want to interview?"

Jaren tried not to be obvious about glancing at her watch, but it was past their regular shift. Again.

"There's only one left on the list, but he'll keep until tomorrow." He felt in need of rejuvenation. "Want to get a drink?"

The suggestion caught her by surprise.

"I'd love to," she told him honestly. Most of the detectives gathered at a local bar, which she'd found to be rather pleasant as well as atmospheric. However, thanks to Kyle, she wasn't her own person anymore. "But I've got someone waiting for me at home."

"Oh."

She saw him withdrawing and realized that he'd misunderstood.

"A certain four-footed furry creature who needs her dinner," she explained, then heard herself suggesting, "We could have a drink at my place. I've got some wine in the refrigerator."

He knew that he should say thanks, but no thanks. Knew that what he needed right now was the noise of a familiar crowd where he could unwind and then go home for perhaps a semi-decent night's sleep.

Even so, Kyle caught himself nodding. "You talked me into it."

The drive to her apartment wasn't far.

Kyle parked within the parking structure, in one of the free spaces near Jaren's assigned space, then followed her to her door.

The second she unlocked it and turned the knob to open the door, a caramel-colored ball of fluff came charging out, launching herself at what she obviously took to be her liberator. Because he was standing to the right of Jaren, Kyle turned out to be the recipient of his namesake's wild enthusiasm.

Kyle picked up the dog and immediately found himself on the receiving end of a madly working pink tongue.

"Hold it, hold it," he laughed, drawing the dog back in order to get a better look at it, and to bring a halt to the impromptu face washing. "She's grown," he said to Jaren.

"They have a habit of doing that," Jaren agreed with a laugh, locking the door behind them.

Very carefully, she removed her service revolver with its holster, placing it next to the microwave oven on the counter.

Kyle put the dog back on the floor and followed suit, depositing his hardware beside hers. With that done, he glanced out toward the living room. The last time he'd been here, the room was filled with towering boxes.

"Looks a lot bigger this way," he commented.

She'd broken down the last of the empty boxes and thrown them in the recycle bin just this past weekend. She smiled now.

"Yeah, I know. Gives Kyle a lot of room to run around. I'd leave the balcony open for her but she's such a friendly dog, she'd probably make a dive down at the first person she sees."

Opening the refrigerator, Jaren reached in and took out the white wine. The bottle, Kyle noted, hadn't been opened yet.

"Saving it for a special occasion?" he asked.

He also took note of the fact that the refrigerator was bare aside from a carton of orange juice.

"Just for my first guest," she answered. "I thought the occasion might be worth celebrating." She glanced at the bottle and noticed the date on it. "2007 was a very good year," she commented, tongue in cheek.

"If you say so." Kyle shrugged. "One year's more or less like another to me."

He didn't elaborate that 2007 was the year his mother had fallen ill. And a little more than a year before the bottom had fallen out of his world when he and his siblings had been told that they'd been fathered by Brian Cavanaugh's older brother, Mike.

After getting the corkscrew, Jaren sank it into the cork and brought the wings down in order to raise it out of the bottle. Meanwhile Kyle, she noticed, had picked up the puppy's small rubber ball and was rolling it to her. The Labrador was overjoyed as she chased after the red object and brought it back to his feet.

Jaren grinned as she took in the game. "You know, you're not nearly the hard-ass you like to pretend you are."

Kyle let the puppy keep the ball and chew on it. He rose to his feet and crossed back to Jaren in the kitchen. "Just ask my brother and sister, they'll tell you otherwise."

She'd always wished that her parents had had more children. She spent a good deal of her childhood yearning for a sibling, someone to share secrets with.

Jaren emptied a can of dog food into the puppy's bowl. She'd barely finished before the Lab came flying over and began eating. With a pleased laugh, she reached into the cabinet directly over the microwave, took out two glasses and set them on the counter.

"What's it like to have two people around who look almost exactly like you?" she asked.

He watched as the puppy polished off her evening meal. "Never gave it much thought. I just see them as individuals." He and his brother hadn't even indulged in the common adolescent prank of switching places. Their voices alone would have given them away. Ethan was far more outgoing than he was, and more soft-spoken. "We've got more differences than similarities," he told her.

Jaren poured two glasses of wine, handed him his and then walked with hers into the living room. She brought along the bottle in case Kyle wanted a refill. One was usually her limit.

Setting the bottle down on the coffee table, she took a seat on the sofa. He sat down next to her. Fed now, the puppy decided that their feet were fair game and curled up happily between them, occasionally raising her head to flick her tongue over Kyle's shoe as a sign of affection.

"Which one's the oldest?" Jaren asked.

"We're triplets," he reminded her.

"I know that, but there's always one that's the oldest. The three of you didn't make your debut at exactly the same time."

"I am," he finally said. Absently, he scratched the puppy's head. The Labrador had shifted over closer toward him. It was clear that she thought of him as the leader of the pack.

"I thought so," Jaren declared. "So, taking charge comes naturally to you."

He didn't like taking charge, just getting things done. His own way. "I'd rather do things alone," he informed her.

"But you don't. You take charge. If a leader's called for, you're it." She saw him frown. He didn't like credit, she concluded. "Nothing to be ashamed of."

"I'm not ashamed," Kyle countered, then took a long sip from his glass. "You're putting me in a niche and I'd rather not be pigeonholed."

She smiled as she took her first sip of wine. "Spoils the mystery?"

He laughed dryly. "There're enough mysteries around right now without that."

Jaren took a breath. Was it her, or had it suddenly gotten warmer? She realized that she was watching his lips as he spoke, letting her mind drift. Maybe the wine was a bad idea, at least for her.

She set the glass down on the table and cleared her throat. "Are you hungry? I can order some pizza," she offered.

He thought of the empty refrigerator. "Was that what you were going to have?" She nodded. "Not exactly a balanced dinner."

"Bread, meat, tomatoes, cheese," she recited the components of her favorite pizza. "Sounds pretty balanced to me." Rising to her feet, she crossed to the kitchen phone and began to dial the number of the local pizza parlor.

Kyle followed her, leaving the glass of wine standing next to hers. "You don't cook, do you?"

She paused for a minute. "Only if I'm looking to come down with food poisoning. Now," she resumed dialing, "what's your pleasure?" The line was busy. She broke the connection and began to dial again.

Kyle wasn't sure just what prompted him to do what he did next. Maybe it was reacting to her question. Maybe it was being alone with her like this and feeling the chemistry crackle between them without the usual distractions of work. And maybe it was the wine and the fact that he hadn't eaten anything in close to eight hours, and then it had only been half a sandwich.

For whatever reason, Kyle took the receiver from her hand and hung it up.

Her mouth turned to pure cotton. Jaren raised her eyes to his. "You want something else besides pizza?" she guessed, the words coming out in almost slow motion. This wasn't what she thought it was, she silent insisted.

*Get a grip. The man just changed his mind about pizza, that's all.*

Taking a breath, Jaren was about to rattle off the names of several other take-out places in the area she'd become familiar with in the last few weeks, but the words never rose to her lips.

Which was just as well because her lips suddenly had something else to deal with. The press of his against them.

Her heart slammed against her chest and she found herself falling into the kiss and the moment. He tasted like no wine she'd ever sampled.

His mouth slanted over hers over and over again, weakening her just a little more with each pass, dissolving her strength and melting her inner core. Struggling to remain grounded, she entwined her arms around his neck, rising up on her toes so that her body could press against his in all the important contact points.

A hunger raced through her, surprising her. She couldn't remember the last time she'd wanted a man to hold her, to kiss her. To make her forget everything else.

She kissed him harder, not wanting to disappear into oblivion without leaving her mark. He responded by tightening his hold on her. She felt a fire ignite in her veins.

This was only going to end one way.

But just as the thought came to her, she could have sworn that music filled the air.

No, not music, ring tones.

Her phone was ringing.

*Oh no, not now.* Jaren wanted to ignore it. With all her heart she wanted to pretend it wasn't ringing, but then she heard another ring tone. Kyle's phone was ringing, too.

The dissonance broke into the moment. A feeling of bereavement, framed in relief, overtook her. This would have been a mistake, she told herself. A glorious, mind-numbing mistake. With reluctance, she pulled back.

"The phones are ringing," Jaren told him needlessly, trying to catch her breath.

She wasn't the only one.

Breathing hard, wondering what the hell had come over him, Kyle nodded and took a step back. He dragged his hand through his dark hair, as if that would somehow restore his thinking process to normal—or as normal as could be expected. Swallowing an unintelligible oath, he pulled out his phone.

Rosetti, he saw, was doing the same with hers. They answered, announcing their names, at almost the exact same time.

"O'Brien."

"Rosetti."

By the way her face paled, Kyle surmised that she was getting the same message that he was. The moment they'd shared was gone as if it had never existed, blown away in the wake of the information they were receiving.

He later remembered thinking that this couldn't be happening. Except that it was. It had.

"When?" he demanded gruffly.

A shaken Riley was on the other end of the line,

calling to tell him that the vampire slayer had struck again. Telling him the slayer's latest victim. Kyle could tell it was all she could do to keep from breaking down. He felt sick to his stomach himself.

"The M.E. hasn't gotten here yet," she was saying. "I called you as soon as I—as we—found the body." He thought he heard a suppressed sob. "Holloway is on the other line, calling Jaren."

"Get a hold of yourself, Riley. Where are you?" he asked gruffly.

It took her a second to remember the names of the streets and get her bearings. When she did, Riley rattled the address off to him.

Kyle didn't bother telling her he'd be right there before he snapped his phone shut. That was a given.

He looked at Jaren who'd already gotten off her cell. She looked even paler than before. He thought of telling her to stay put, but that would have been playing favorites. Most likely, she'd just resent him for it.

"You okay?" His voice was harsh as he grappled with the situation himself.

Feeling like someone in a surreal nightmare, Jaren nodded, then added in a haunted voice, "I've been better." Pivoting on her heel, she crossed to the counter and picked up her weapon. She strapped it on quickly.

Maybe Holloway had made a mistake, she thought desperately. Maybe, but even as she tried to advance the desperate notion, she knew she was wrong. There was no mistake.

"Let's go," she cried, hurrying out the door before Kyle.

* * *

With sirens blaring, flying through all the lights, they lost no time getting to the back alley where the slayer's latest victim lay. Jaren approached the body on legs that grew progressively more rubbery.

Detective Diego Sanchez, his dark hair slicked back, wearing the black all-weather coat he favored, died with a surprised look on his face. A copy of *The Vampire Diaries* lay on the ground several feet away from him.

There was a stake through his heart.

Kyle crouched down beside the body. He looked at the book. It was facedown on the pavement, its spine broken and flat. Was that what did it? Had the book attracted his killer? Or was it the way Sanchez liked to dress? Kyle struggled against feeling sick.

He rose to his feet. "What's he doing with this book?" he demanded. The question was addressed to anyone who could give him an answer.

Holloway sighed heavily. He and Sanchez had been partnered for the last six years. For the purposes of the investigation, Kyle had assigned each of them to one of the other detectives on the task force, to give them the benefit of their experience.

"He said he wanted to know what all the fuss was about. Thought it might help him to figure out the inner workings of his girlfriend's mind," Holloway finally said, standing over the body and shaking his head. "Damn it, who's going to tell his mother?"

"I'll do it," Kyle said, his voice low, barely a rumble.

Holloway looked at him. "I didn't mean for you—"

Kyle cut him off. "My task force, my job," he said with finality. Forcing himself to focus on the crime, he scanned the area. None of this made any sense. Why Sanchez?

"Anyone know what he was doing tonight?"

Riley cleared her throat. Sanchez had been assigned to her. "He told me he was playing a hunch," she volunteered.

Kyle turned to look at the woman who, thanks to his mother's deathbed revelation, had become part of his family. "Which was?"

Riley shook her head. "He wouldn't tell me. He said—" Her voice cracked and she began again. "He said that if it didn't pan out, he didn't want to be left with egg on his face. I told him I'd go with him, but he said there was no point in both of us chasing this down." Riley pressed her lips together as if trying to force down the tears. "I should have gone with him."

Unable to witness her guilt a second longer, Jaren came up to her and tried to put her arms around the woman. Riley shook her off, then caved.

"You had no way of knowing what was going to happen," Jaren told her.

There was anguish in Riley's eyes as she said, "That's exactly why I should have gone."

"Don't waste time beating yourself up," Kyle told her. "We've got a killer to catch. Riley, I want you to find out all the calls Sanchez made on his cell phone in the last twenty-four hours. Maybe we can figure out where he was going tonight."

Riley nodded. "On it."

"Holloway, go with her," he ordered, and then looked at the three detectives in the alley. "From now on, I don't want anyone going off on their own."

"We can work faster if we split up," Holloway argued.

"No one is going alone," Kyle repeated with feeling. "Do I make myself clear?"

"Clear," Riley agreed, her voice hardly above a tortured whisper.

"He wasn't killed here," Jaren realized, just as the M.E. arrived. When the others turned to her, she explained. "There's no pool of blood. He was killed somewhere else and then brought here."

*Why?* Kyle wondered. Had the crime scene been too close to the slayer's home? "I still want a canvas of the area. See if anyone saw or heard something. A truck, a van, a car pulling into the alley and then leaving." Even as he said it, he knew it was too much to hope for.

"Tire marks do?" Holloway asked.

Kyle felt his pulse jump. "Fresh?" he asked, hurrying over to where Holloway stood.

Jaren had already joined the other detective and squatted down to examine the markings. "Looks to be," she answered.

"Have CSI run down the make and model," Kyle instructed. He could see the team members entering the alley. "Maybe our vampire slayer made his first mistake."

"His first mistake," Riley said grimly, "was killing one of our own."

No one argued that point.

# Chapter 12

"I'm going with you," Jaren informed Kyle as she hurried to catch up to him outside of the alley.

Kyle shook his head. "I'm on my way to see Sanchez's mother."

Of all the things that a police officer did, Kyle thought, informing a parent or spouse of their loved one's death had to be among the worst. Even he wasn't immune to it, despite the fact that he did his best to distance himself from the people he worked with.

Jaren lengthened her stride to keep pace with him. "I know."

Kyle stopped abruptly. "Thanks, but I don't need someone to hold my hand. I've done this more times than I care to remember."

"Everyone needs someone to hold their hand once in a while," Jaren told him. No matter how aloof he pretended to be, she knew Sanchez's murder had gotten to him just like it had to the rest of them. Having to tell the man's mother the detective had been slain was going to be hard enough with support. She didn't want him doing it alone. "I'm coming with you so you might as well get used to it. Besides, Mrs. Sanchez might want a woman there."

He didn't want to waste time arguing, especially since he had a feeling that he was not about to win. Rosetti seemed the type to argue the ears off a brass monkey. And maybe she was right. Maybe having a woman there might give Sanchez's mother some measure of comfort, although if it were him, there would simply be no way to glean comfort from this kind of a situation.

Kyle resumed walking to his vehicle. They were parked one behind the other. "If you're going to come, let's go."

They drove separately, just as they had from her apartment. She hadn't thought to ask him for Mrs. Sanchez's address, so perforce, she had to follow closely behind him when all she wanted was to open up the engine and go fast. The tension she was experiencing reached critical mass.

The porch light was on at the Sanchez residence but the lights inside were off. Kyle seemed to hesitate, not wanting to wake the woman up to news like this. But in the end, he finally pressed the doorbell.

Several minutes went by before a light went on inside the house and they heard the lock being flipped open. Jaren heard Kyle take in a breath as the door opened.

Inez Sanchez was a short woman whose full-figured frame testified to her love of food. At sixty-three, her face was unlined and only a few gray strands had found their way into her midnight black hair.

Her dark eyes were still sleepy as she recognized the young man at her door. She smiled a sleepy greeting.

"Diego isn't home yet," she told him.

"I know," Kyle replied.

The two words erased the woman's smile. Horror took its place as her eyes widened.

"Oh no, no. Please, no."

Kyle forced the words out. "Mrs. Sanchez, I'm so very sorry to have to tell you this, but—"

"No. *Es la mentira.* No. He is coming home. Diego is coming home. He is just late," she insisted, looking from her son's friend to the young woman who had come with him. Her eyes begged them to tell her she wasn't wrong.

"He isn't late," Kyle said, raising his voice above her cries. "He's dead."

Mrs. Sanchez's eyes were wild as she heard the words that brought the end of hope in her life. Her knees buckled, refusing to hold her up. Kyle caught her, but it was Jaren who moved in, Jaren who put her arms around the woman and held her close. Mrs. Sanchez struggled, trying to shrug her off. Jaren refused to let her, holding on tightly until the detective's mother finally dissolved into a pool of tears.

In her misery, Inez Sanchez completely reverted to her native tongue. Kyle was surprised when he heard Jaren answer her.

Jaren said every soothing thing she could think of and then fervently swore to the woman that they would get the man who killed her son. She sealed her promise by taking an oath on her father's grave.

It was the latter vow that finally got through to the grieving mother and stilled her louder sobs.

At a loss, feeling as if he was in the way, Kyle quietly slipped out of the small, single-story stucco house.

Jaren was aware of his leaving, but her attention was focused on Inez.

She remained with Mrs. Sanchez another twenty minutes, until, utterly exhausted, the woman fell into a fitful sleep on the sofa. Taking out one of her newly printed cards, Jaren wrote a note on the back, urging the woman to call her anytime if she needed to talk. Time of day or night didn't matter.

She left the card propped up against the base of the lamp on the end table. With an aching heart, she tiptoed outside and quietly pulled the door shut behind her. She made sure she heard the lock click into place.

When she turned around, Jaren bit back a scream. Her nerves were closer to the surface than she thought.

"You didn't go home," she said needlessly. When he slipped out, she was certain Kyle had taken the opportunity to go home himself.

"I said we were supposed to do things in pairs, remember? I'm not about to have you out on the streets at this hour. Especially in this neighborhood. It's not safe." He nodded toward the house behind her. "She going to be all right?"

Jaren shook her head. "Not for a good long while," she guessed. "But she cried herself into exhaustion and fell asleep. I left her on the sofa. Sleep's the best thing for her right now. Is there anyone we can call for her?"

"Not that I know of." He led the way back to the cars parked at the curb. "Get in your car," he instructed. "I'll follow you home."

"Then what, I'll follow you to your place to make sure you got in safely?"

Kyle frowned at her. Why did everything have to turn into a debate? "I'm a man."

"So was Sanchez," she reminded him grimly. "Seems to me that this maniac only goes after men."

"So far," Kyle pointed out.

She stifled a shiver. O'Brien might be right, but she hoped not. There was already enough panic about this killer without bringing the female population into it.

Jaren couldn't remember ever feeling this restless, this unsettled. She wouldn't be able to sleep tonight. Not given the way she felt.

"There's no point in going back to my apartment," she told him. "I won't sleep. I'm too keyed up."

She was about to say that she might as well go to the precinct and see if she could get any work done, when she heard him say, "I'll come with you. We can talk until you wind down."

He'd surprised her again. Just when she thought she had him pegged. "Okay," she agreed, although she had her doubts that she would be able to unwind. She felt like a cherry bomb about to go off.

* * *

"I didn't know you spoke Spanish," Kyle commented as they walked to her door.

"I can get by," she said modestly. "My best friend in elementary school was Mexican. I liked hanging around her house after school." She smiled as a few memories came back to her. Jaren put her key in the lock and opened her door. "Her mother made the greatest meals."

"What about your mother?" He waited for her to enter, then followed her inside.

Jaren turned on the light switch beside the door. The light came on in her kitchen. Sprawled out on the kitchen floor, the puppy raised her head to see who was intruding into her home. Recognizing them, the Labrador came bounding over, greeting both as if they'd all been separated for months rather than hours.

"My mother tended toward getting takeout and frozen dinners," Jaren remembered. She picked up the puppy and gave her a hug.

"I guess the apple didn't fall far from the tree," Kyle speculated.

"The apple had better things to do than to experiment in the kitchen," she informed him. Between taking care of her father, keeping house for him and going to school, she had little time to be a teenager, much less a chef with a learning curve. "One day when I was twelve, my mother decided she could do better." She tried to sound flippant, but even so, the memory hurt. "I came home from school and found a note from her on the kitchen table, telling me she was sorry but she was dying by inches living her life. She asked me to take care of my father, saying I'd probably do a better job than she did."

He waited for her to continue. When she didn't, he asked, "And that was it?"

The note was the last communication she had with her mother. "That was it."

He found himself feeling sorry for the child she had been. That was a hell of a burden to place on a twelve-year-old's shoulders. "What did your father do when he found out?"

She did what she could to distance herself from the memory. As much as she loved her father, she was keenly aware of his shortcomings.

"Went out and bought another bottle of vodka." There was a bittersweet smile on her lips. Thoughts of her father always evoked a feeling of affection and protectiveness, mingled with guilt because she was so disappointed that he didn't try harder to get away from his demons. The demons that eventually took him away from her. "That was pretty much my father's solution to everything. Vodka. Black Russians were his favorite." And then, because she knew how that sounded, she quickly added, "He really tried to be a good father, but he just wasn't strong enough."

Her words came back to her. Jaren looked at Kyle, just a bit stunned. "How did we wind up talking about my father?"

"Doesn't matter." He watched her for a long moment. "You were right."

The compliment came out of nowhere. In order to savor it, she needed to know its origins. "About?"

"About coming with me to break the news to Mrs. Sanchez. I wouldn't have been able to handle her without you. Thanks," he concluded.

"Can't cook but knows how to comfort people on the receiving end of bad news," she declared, lowering her voice to sound as if she was narrating her good points. And then she smiled. "We all have our skills."

Again, he looked at her for a long moment, but this time, he caught himself experiencing the same pull he had before the awful call about Sanchez's murder had come through.

What was there about this woman that pulled him in like that? That tangled up his ordinarily straight thought process?

"Some," he said, combing his fingers through her hair, "have more than others."

Jaren felt her heart race again. Even harder than the first time. The same wave of warmth overtook her. But this time, she didn't even bother trying to avoid it. This time, she wanted to race to it. She *needed* the contact. Needed to feel human again.

This wasn't about forming an attachment or nurturing a relationship, she told herself. It was just teeth-jarring, unrelenting physical attraction. She didn't want to think for a space of time. More than anything, she just wanted to wipe away the image of Sanchez in the alley. Wanted to wipe out the sound of Mrs. Sanchez's sobs that still rang in her ears.

She took the plunge. Someone had to go first and she couldn't count on him. He was probably more grounded.

"Make love with me, O'Brien," she whispered as she laced her arms around his neck. "Nobody has to know. Just make me stop thinking."

Kyle knew he should disengage himself from her. Knew that he should say something about being her superior on this case and that they had a professional relationship to maintain. They were coworkers and these kinds of things—even if it was only a onetime thing— rarely worked out. He wasn't in the market for a relationship, and a one-night stand with a fellow detective just wasn't a good idea.

But for the life of him, he couldn't voice a single protest, couldn't put a single thought into words. He was only aware of the overwhelming desire pulsing within him.

He wanted her.

Wanted to make love with her until they were both mindless and cleansed.

Kyle struggled to verbalize a protest for both their own good, but he lost the battle before it ever began.

Jaren sealed her lips to his and suddenly, there was nothing else but her and the passion roaring through his veins like a runaway freight train.

The moment her lips touched his, Kyle found himself lost in a sea of passion. Passion of a magnitude that took his breath away. Never would he have even entertained the thought that he was capable of feeling something like this.

He gave himself up to it.

Clothes went flying as they stumbled from the kitchen to the living room, desperate for the feel of skin, for the hot sizzle of flesh on flesh.

Maybe her bedroom was the ultimate goal, but if so, they didn't get there in time.

Their bodies were naked before they were halfway there.

Over and over Kyle brought his mouth to hers as his hands familiarized themselves with all the inviting contours of her supple, firm body. He could feel himself reacting to the way she raked her hands over him. Everything within Kyle hummed with anticipation.

He wouldn't have been able to say who wanted this more, if he did or if it was she. In the end, he supposed it turned out to be a draw.

They both won.

Sinking to the floor, they were oblivious to the yipping of the puppy that kept excitedly circling them. The Labrador undoubtedly thought this was some sort of new game.

But if this was a game, it carried incredibly high stakes. His very soul depended on this, on losing himself within the sweet fire that she had created within his veins. Capturing both her wrists in his hand, Kyle raised them above her head as he pleasured her, pleasured himself savaging her mouth.

When he could feel her heart hammering against his, he allowed his mouth to roam, to take a swift detour along her throat, her breasts, her quivering abdomen.

And with each pass of his lips, his teeth, his tongue, he could feel Jaren twisting and turning beneath him, eagerly absorbing every nuance, every second of sweet agony he created for her.

Her very movement against his body both fed the hunger and made it more intense within him.

Breaking free of his hold, Jaren grabbed hold of his shoulders and urgently tugged on them, finally succeeding in pulling him back up to her until they were face-to-face with one another.

He saw his destiny in her eyes. It would have scared the hell out of him had he been thinking clearly.

But he wasn't.

He was feeling and that made for a world of difference.

An urgency drummed through every fiber of his being as he drove himself into her. Filling her and nullifying a void within himself.

At least for the moment.

The frantic rhythm of hips against hips increased until they reached the final peak. He groaned as the exploding sensation momentarily stole him away from everything else.

Kyle tightened his arms around her, as if to hold the feeling close for just a second longer. But even so, it was vanishing.

Moving off Jaren, he rolled onto his back, one arm tucked beneath his head. He was surprised to discover that his other arm was curved around her.

What the hell did that mean?

He was too drained to try to figure it out. Too drained

even to reclaim his arm. He let it remain until his breathing became regular again.

With effort, he recalled her last words to him. "Well, did it make you stop thinking?" he asked her in a low, hoarse whisper.

Jaren didn't answer. She *couldn't* answer. Her breathing was completely erratic. If she spoke right now, she'd squeak.

God, what had happened here? She knew she'd been the one to start this, to actually ask for it, but she certainly hadn't expected this degree of passion, this degree of *anything* to erupt within her. Granted, she hadn't been with many men, but nothing like this had *ever* happened to her before.

Pressing her lips together, Jaren took a breath, desperate to make light of a situation that was anything but light. She instinctively knew, without being told, that to do anything else—to attach any importance to what had just happened, to even allude to the possibility that this was the start of something rather than solely a onetime thing—would scare the hell out of Kyle.

It certainly did out of her.

She took another breath, hoping her voice wouldn't crack. "I can't even remember my name, rank and serial number," she quipped.

"Funny," he told her, turning his head slightly to look at her, "I can."

He felt her breasts brush against him as she turned her body to his. Her expression was serious. "I meant what I said."

His mind was a complete blank. Not a usual state for him. What was it that she had said? Had he even heard her? "About?"

"About no one needing to know about what happened here. I just—" She stumbled, searching for the right words. "—just wanted to forget."

"Hypnosis would have been less exhausting," he told her so matter-of-factly, for a moment, Jaren thought he was serious. And then she saw a glimmer of amusement in his eyes. Why that ushered in relief was something she wasn't able to explain.

"You have a sense of humor." Now there was something she wouldn't have accused him of harboring.

He laughed shortly. There was a time, he recalled, when he was quick to laugh. Before he discovered that life wasn't funny, it was a challenge. "Don't let it get around."

She smiled, running her fingers along the outline of his biceps. He was doing it again, she thought, reaching out to something inside of her. She wondered if he knew. Probably not. If he knew, he'd stop. He struck her as a man who didn't like complications.

"Your secret's safe with me," she promised. To bring the point home, she crossed her heart with her finger.

Moving her hand, he pressed a kiss to her breast. "As long as we're keeping secrets," he said softly, turning his body toward hers.

She could feel the fire starting again. Could feel the desire taking hold again. Suddenly, she wanted to lose herself in him just one more time.

"Yes?"

He didn't answer her. At least, not verbally. Instead, he began to make love with her again. Except far more languidly this time.

He was certain that he had missed areas the first time around because they had gone at it with such a furor. But a woman like Jaren deserved to be made love with slowly, underscoring every movement. And he had no idea what possessed him, but he fully intended to be the one who did it.

# Chapter 13

Jaren woke up several minutes before her alarm, the smell of coffee teasing its way into her consciousness.

More specifically, the smell of coffee, bacon and toast.

Staring at the ceiling, her mind trying to focus, Jaren thought she was dreaming. And then she remembered Kyle and last night and was certain that she was still asleep.

But the aroma persisted, so she finally sat up. And realized that she was naked. She slapped down the buzzer as it began to ring. Maybe last night hadn't been a dream after all.

Getting up, Jaren quickly threw on a pair of shorts and a T-shirt, then went to the kitchen to investigate the source of the aroma.

She found Kyle standing by the stove with his name-sake sitting up at his feet. The latter was leaving drool marks on the floor, hoping for a taste of what smelled so temptingly good.

Kyle glanced over his shoulder. "You're up."

Her mouth curved. Now here was a sight she never imagined in her kitchen. "You do magic."

Kyle tried to place her comment in context. "If you're referring to last night, you were pretty inspiring yourself."

She felt a blush rushing over her fair skin, turning it a soft shade of warm. "I meant breakfast. You're cooking."

He looked back at the frying pan on the stove. "Oh, yeah."

Her head still jumbled, she tried to make her statement understood. "All I had in the refrigerator was wine and orange juice. You make eggs, toast and bacon appear?"

He laughed, finally understanding her confusion. She probably thought if he was going to go out for break-fast, he would return with a paper bag with a fast-food logo embossed on its side. "I went to the grocery store. You sleep pretty soundly."

"I had one hell of a workout last night."

There was a hint of a smile on his lips as Kyle peered at her over his shoulder again. "Yeah, come to think of it, me, too."

For a second, the only sound in the room was the siz-zle of the bacon. Jaren tightened her lips. "Is this going to be the awkward part?"

Silence had never bothered him. At times, it was a

welcomed companion, a place to seek shelter. "Not unless you want it to be."

Hunger got the better of her. She could see why the Labrador was drooling. "What I want is to sample what you've just made."

Kyle turned off the heat and moved both frying pans to cool burners. "That's what it's here for," he told her.

Two empty plates sat on the counter and he divided the contents of both frying pans. A second later, toast joined each serving.

Jaren carried the plates to the table while he brought up the rear, a cup of coffee in each hand. Without realizing it, he watched the soft sway of her hips as she walked, appreciation filtering through him.

She didn't wait for him, but started eating as he took his seat opposite her. "This is good," Jaren pronounced with feeling.

He shrugged off her compliment. "Kind of hard to spoil scrambled eggs." Breaking off a piece of bacon, Kyle held it out to the eager puppy. It disappeared in a heartbeat. She licked his fingers several times over to get every last bit of flavor off them.

"Not so hard, trust me," she countered, and then smiled. "It seems that you've got more than one hidden talent."

He raised his eyes to hers and smiled himself, not saying anything. Some things were better left without a comment.

Not wanting to let on that last night had shaken up his world as much as it had, Kyle moved the conversation toward the case while they ate. He was now convinced that they were dealing with a psychopath and that the vampire angle was the one to follow.

"After all," he said, draining his coffee cup, "Son of Sam swore he was getting his instructions from his dog. There's no reason to doubt that our killer went off the deep end and now thinks he's getting his orders from some *higher power* telling him to kill *vampires*."

She wasn't so sure she went along with the second half of his theory. "And that higher power is identifying the vampires for him?"

He fed a little of his toast to the dog. Jaren pretended not to notice, but the fact that he did warmed her heart even more. "Sounds good to me," Kyle said.

"By higher power, you mean the voices he might be hearing in his head?"

After he finished eatomg, he wiped his mouth with the napkin. "That's what I mean."

She followed his line of reasoning. "So, you think it's just random."

Kyle nodded. "Easier that way. And," he reminded her, "they did have the book in common."

"They had more than that in common," she countered. "They had the killer. There has to be some kind of connection between the neurosurgeon and the CEO that were killed." She hurried to explain her reasoning. "The killer had to physically see those books in their offices. He didn't plant them like a calling card. They were what set him off." She'd bet a year's salary on it. "Which consequently means he knew the men. He knew them well enough to get admitted into their offices."

"And Sanchez?" Kyle asked. "How do you factor in his murder?"

The mention of the detective vividly brought back his mother's anguish. Jaren did what she could to shut it out. Remembering would do no one any good right now. "The killer must have interacted with Sanchez."

Kyle followed her reasoning to its logical conclusion. "Which means that, technically, we've met the killer. Or at least Sanchez did. He's got to be one of the people who was interviewed."

"That's what I think." Finishing her breakfast, she retired her fork and took one last sip of her coffee. "What about the Count?"

That was the least complicated of the murders. "Wrong place at the wrong time," Kyle guessed. "Maybe the Count just crossed the killer's path. Or maybe the killer knew him, too. Hard to say but you're right, the murders weren't done at random."

"Nice to be in agreement," she commented. Rising, Jaren brought both plates over to the sink. "You're the guest so you can have the shower first."

He placed the two coffee cups next to the stacked dishes in the sink. "There's a drought on," he reminded her.

Nothing new there, she thought. California had been tottering on the brink of a drought for years now. The governor had just made it official. Turning around to look at Kyle, she wasn't sure just where he was going with this.

"I suppose we can both walk through a car wash but that might cause too much of a commotion."

Kyle fought back the urge to fold his arms around her. He had no idea just what was going on. Displays of affection were not what he was about, yet something had definitely happened last night—something that changed him.

"I was thinking more along the lines of showering together." He watched as the smile bloomed on Jaren's face.

"Showering together," she repeated. When he nodded, she laughed. "You are a constant source of surprise to me, O'Brien."

"Yeah, me, too," he confessed.

Without another word, she linked her fingers with his and led him to the bathroom.

When they arrived at the precinct an hour later, the lieutenant told Kyle that Brian Cavanaugh wanted everyone to gather together in the conference room.

As the various detectives and officers filed in the mood was somber. The usual banter and jokes were conspicuously absent. It hadn't taken long for word to spread and Sanchez's murder was on everyone's mind.

When the room was full, Brian went to the front beside the bulletin board and began.

"As you all know, Detective Diego Sanchez was murdered last night, the latest victim of the so-called vampire slayer." He scanned the sea of faces, some mourning, some angry. None were indifferent. The killer had hit them where they lived. "I don't have to tell you that this case has now taken priority over everything else. I am authorizing extra hours, extra manpower.

Whatever we need, we get in order to bring this psychopath in. Alive, if possible," he stressed. "Nobody is going off the reservation on this. I want no loose cannons, do I make myself clear?"

Muttered affirmative responses came from around the room.

Brian addressed each and every one. "There'll be no vacations, no time off until this case is solved and Detective Sanchez's killer is brought to justice."

Kyle raised his hand. When Brian nodded, he asked, "What about Sanchez's funeral? Does anyone know about the arrangements?"

"Not yet," Brian told him. "I'm going to go see Mrs. Sanchez as soon I finish here. There'll be a notice posted with all the information when I find out." He took a breath. Since he'd taken on the mantle of chief of detectives, not a single detective had died while on duty. This had hit him as hard as it had any of them. "According to my information, Sanchez's mother is a widow and he was her only child. I'm sure that all of you will find some time to stop by her home and pay your respects. The woman is going to need an awful lot of emotional support. Okay," he announced, "now let's go get that bastard."

As the others began to file out, Brian turned toward his stepdaughter. "Walk with me, Riley," he urged, leaving the conference room.

Startled by the sound of his voice, Riley turned to face him. "Sure, Chief. You want to talk to me?"

Brian nodded. Married to his former partner, Lila McIntyre, for less than six months, he was still trying to work out the logistics of taking on four stepchildren in addition to his own four grown children.

Part of this involved trying to arrive at what to be called by Lila's children, children he'd watched grow up into fine adults as well as law-enforcement agents. He might be their chief of detectives, but first and foremost, he was their stepfather and he intended to be more of a father than their real one had been. For the most part, he'd unofficially held the role for years now.

Walking out into the hall with Riley, he took her aside and, concerned, asked, "Are you all right?"

"Sure."

The assurance came out much too quickly, like an automatic response when someone asked a stranger about their health. "According to what I heard, you were the one who discovered Sanchez's body and called the others."

He watched as Riley unconsciously clenched her hands at her sides. As if steeling herself off from the memory. "Yes, I was."

His manner was completely sympathetic. "That had to be hard on you."

Riley raised her chin defensively. "I've seen dead bodies before, Chief."

He saw through her. "But you never shared a police vehicle with one of them. Never went out to lunch with one of them," he pointed out. "What I'm saying, Riley, is if you need some time off—"

She looked at him in surprise. "I thought you said that nobody's to take any time off until this guy's behind bars."

"That was a pep talk for the team," he clarified. "And for the most part, I meant it. But I'm not about to drive any of my people to the point that they snap. That includes you."

"That's favoritism," she protested.

"No," he contradicted, "that's just being a good leader. I'm not concerned because you're my stepdaughter, I'm concerned because you're one of my detectives, and I'm not about to sacrifice you or any of the other detectives to solve this case. We can do that without incurring any more casualties," he said pointedly. "Now, if you need—"

Riley shook her head. "I appreciate what you're trying to do, but what I need right now is to have that lowlife sitting in a jail cell, contemplating getting a needle in his arm."

Brian suppressed a sigh. Riley was just as stubborn as her mother. "If you're sure…"

"I'm sure." She forced a smile to her lips. "But thanks for asking—Dad."

Being addressed that way obviously pleased him. Brian smiled at his wife's younger daughter. "Okay, the first sign of *battle fatigue* and I'm pulling you out. Understood?"

"Understood," she answered solemnly. A little of her smile reached her eyes as she said, "I always told Mom you were a good guy. Now, if you'll excuse me, I've got work to do."

Brian nodded. He had to get going himself. He'd promised Lila that he would stop by to pick her up. She insisted on going with him to pay their respects to Sanchez's mother.

Parting with Riley, he walked toward the elevators. Even with his wife at his side, he knew this was going to be difficult.

There were days that he liked being chief of detectives less than others.

The funeral was held in the morning three days later. The sky was properly overcast, threatening a cloudburst that never materialized. Every detective and police officer from the Aurora Police Department turned out for the ceremony. This was only the third time in twenty-eight years that a police officer had died in the line of duty. Sanchez's murder left its imprint on each and every one of them.

In the church, Brian and his wife were on one side of Mrs. Sanchez, and Andrew and his wife, Rose, sat on her other, silently offering their support. There was no shortage of people to eulogize the fallen detective. By the time the ceremony was over, there wasn't a dry eye or an uncommitted heart left in the entire church.

The solemnity accompanied them all as they returned to the precinct and their duties.

The phones had been ringing off the hook and there was no shortage of *tips* to follow up on. True to his word, Brian had provided extra man power in order to track them all down.

But they were no closer to cracking the case than they had been three days ago.

\* \* \*

That afternoon, though he loathed to do it, Kyle had to temporarily put his part in the investigation on hold. A case he'd worked on over a year ago had finally reached the trial stage and he was due in court to give his testimony.

Before he left, he stopped at Jaren's desk. "I want you to stay here and go over the testimonies we've gotten in. See if you can find inconsistencies."

Busy work, she thought. He was giving her busy work. He couldn't possibly want her to stay at her desk, reading through reams of reports.

"Wouldn't it be better if I just talked to these people again? People tend to slip up when they talk."

"Only if you get someone to go with you," he cautioned. "I was serious about nobody going off alone. We're too much of a target. The killer knows us, we don't know him."

Everyone around her was out on the field. They'd lost no time right after the funeral.

"How about if I dress up like Rebecca of Sunnybrook Farm? No mistaking me for a threatening vampire then."

Kyle frowned at her. "I'm not taking a chance on losing any more people. Just stay put," were his parting words to her.

Inside, she fumed, but she nodded. "Can I go to the bathroom by myself?" she called out as he crossed to the door.

"No."

She muttered under her breath as she went back to the

stacks of notes she'd taken. Wading through the combined names of interviewees and reviewing their connections to the first two victims, she found no overlaps.

The only name that was even remotely connected to both victims turned out to be a dead man. Not only that, but Jackson Massey had died before either one of the victims had.

Still, since it was the *only* name connected to both victims, Jaren decided to do a little more digging into the man's past. Part of her felt as if she was spinning her wheels but then, most police work was just that, working blindly, hoping for a breakthrough against all odds.

Availing herself of various newspaper archives that were stored on the Internet, she discovered that the late billionaire was a dynamic man who made his mark in the world early in life. He'd earned his first billion before he turned twenty-five and was regarded as a golden boy by his contemporaries.

But despite his incredible good fortune and keen business acumen, his life was not without its tragedies. The young wife he adored died when her appendix ruptured while they were vacationing in a remote part of Africa. She died while being transported by helicopter to the closest hospital. That was scarcely a year after Massey's twin sons were born.

As she continued reading, she found that the twins became the focal point of a statewide search when they were kidnapped at the age of four. Though the FBI had been called in, Massey himself actually rescued Finley, the only surviving twin. His brother, Derek, had accidentally been killed just a few hours before Jackson and his hired mercenaries had stormed the kidnapper's hiding place.

They'd talked to Finley, she recalled while going over the list of the neurosurgeon's patients. This was what had been nagging at her that first time. She remembered reading about this!

Questions began forming in her head.

Jaren managed to unearth some rather choppy footage that had appeared on national news stations right after the rescue. Jackson emerging from a run-down, abandoned warehouse in San Francisco, holding his son in his arms. Finley had his face buried in his father's chest, frightened by all the attention.

When one zealous reporter shoved a microphone at the boy and asked if his captor had hurt him, Jaren thought she heard Finley utter a single, muffled word. "Monsters."

Curious, she searched for more details on the rescue.

Most of what she discovered was repetitive but eventually, she found something more. It was an interview with Finley conducted on the fifteenth anniversary of his rescue. In it, he freely praised his father, once again calling Jackson his hero. She remembered that was what he'd said when grieving over his father's death. Finley went on to describe how, at four, he'd thought his kidnapper was a demon, a vampire who had killed his twin and that his father had slain him.

The word *slain* jumped out at her.

Jackson Massey had, in fact, told the police that he had been forced to shoot the man holding his son captive. The kidnapper never regained consciousness and had died before the ambulance arrived. None of the men who had been hired by Massey to help find his son contradicted his story.

Jaren felt a rush of adrenaline as she reread the article. The words *vampire* and *slain* stood out in huge neon lights.

# Chapter 14

Jaren struggled not to get too excited.

*This had to be it.*

But even as she thought this, she told herself that stumbling across the article was almost too good to be true. However, every so often, things *did* fall into place, Jaren thought, and miracles *did* happen.

She looked at the article again, skimming it from beginning to end. Finley Massey *did* have a connection to both the neurosurgeon and the CEO, the vampire slayer's first two victims. All right, the connection was an indirect one through his father, Jackson, but even so, it was legitimate.

And Sanchez had talked to him at least once.

She needed to talk to Finley Massey face-to-face again.

During the first interview, when she and O'Brien were going down the list of the neurosurgeon's patients, she remembered that the young man had struck her as unstable. But then, she cut him a little slack because his father had just passed away. She vividly remembered what it was like for her those first few weeks after her father was gone. She had difficulty finding her place in life until she could finally redefine herself in new terms. If you loved a parent—she suspected that whether he was a billionaire or a fragile human being—the feeling of emptiness and being abandoned was the same.

What if Finley actually *was* unbalanced? And more than just a little bit. What if Finley blamed the surgeon for his father's death and had gone to confront the man in his office? Maybe the shock of his father's passing had unhinged Massey and when he saw the copy of the vampire book on the doctor's desk, that had sent him over the edge.

She knew it sounded a little bit far-fetched but right now, there wasn't anything else to go with. All the tips that had been called in by an eager-to-help public had gone nowhere.

Looking around, Jaren realized that she was still the only one in the conference room. Everyone else was partnered up and out in the field.

As she reached for her oversize purse, Kyle's parting words replayed themselves in her head: "Nobody goes out alone."

Indecision rippled through her.

If she waited for someone to show up, she could

very well lose an opportunity. If Finley took off for some reason, or killed someone else, she would never forgive herself.

Damn it, she wasn't some naive, vulnerable college freshman, she was a police detective, skilled at defending the public as well as herself. She couldn't just sit here, twiddling her thumbs until someone showed up to hold her hand on this detail.

Torn, Jaren glanced toward the doorway. She wasn't about to go in search of another detective and ask him or her to accompany her on an interview like some second grader who needed a partner in order to take the hall pass and go to the bathroom.

But if she went on her own, Kyle would be furious.

Since when did that matter?

Maybe Kyle was finished testifying. If he was, then he could meet her at the Massey estate.

Mentally crossing her fingers, Jaren pressed the keypad with the number to his cell phone. The second the connection was made, it immediately went to voice mail. She frowned, listening to the recording. This could only mean one thing. His phone was off.

Most likely, he was still in the courthouse since all cells were required to be turned off.

Frustrated, she exhaled slowly. And then she had an idea. She decided to cover her tail and leave Kyle a message just in case he did get out early and came back to the precinct. If he saw that she was gone, she knew he'd assume the worst and this time, he'd be right. But if she left him a message, then she was in the clear. Sort of.

"O'Brien, I think I just might have found us a lead. No, scratch that, I think I've solved the case. Finley Massey and his twin brother were kidnapped when they were four years old. His brother didn't survive the ordeal. The kidnapper accidentally killed him. When Finley was rescued—FYI, by his father and a band of mercenaries Massey'd hired—the four-year-old said that monsters, specifically *vampires*," she emphasized, "had killed his brother. Little footnote, the twins were kidnapped on Halloween while making their trick-or-treat rounds with their nanny. Could be that the kidnapper was disguised as Count Dracula. Gives you chills, doesn't it?" she asked. God knows, it did her. "I know this isn't going to exactly thrill you, but I'm going to go to the estate to talk to Massey again."

Anticipating what O'Brien would say to this piece of information, she added in a slightly lower, more seductive voice, "I'm a big girl—as I think you've already figured out." The next moment, O'Brien's voice mail cut her off. She'd exceeded her time limit.

So be it, Jaren thought, flipping her phone closed and tucking it back into her pocket.

*Please let it be Finley,* she thought as she double-checked the address to the Massey estate. Grabbing her purse, she left.

Jaren was out of the room, and halfway down the hall on her way to the elevator when she suddenly stopped and retraced her steps. Going to her desk, she opened the bottom drawer and took out the copy of *The Vampire Diaries*. She'd never bothered to take it home. Questioning Finley Massey might not get her anywhere, but if he saw the book in her possession, that just might trigger something in his head. At least, she fervently hoped so.

Kathy Hubert, the housekeeper who opened the door, instantly recognized her from the previous two visits to the estate. It was obvious that the woman wasn't happy to see her. According to what she had read, Kathy was a long-time employee of the Massey family.

This time, the housekeeper didn't even stand on ceremony or pretend to be polite. "Why can't you leave the boy alone?" she asked. She remained standing in the doorway and blocking any access into the mansion like a short, squat avenging angel.

"The *boy*," Jaren reminded her politely, "is over thirty. And I've got more questions for him. There's been another murder," she added, certain that the woman already knew that. There was no way to avoid the broadcasts unless you didn't watch TV. The all-news stations talked about nothing else.

"There've been lots of murders in this city," the housekeeper retorted stubbornly. She crossed her arms before her ample bosom. "And none of them have anything to do with Mr. Finley." Her complexion reddened with anger. "If Mr. Jackson was still alive—"

"None of this might be happening," Jaren speculated, but for a far different reason. "Now can I see Mr. Massey please, or do I have to arrest you for obstructing justice?"

The housekeeper's brown eyes narrowed and she snorted in disgust. "This way, please."

Kathy Hubert turned on her short, sensible squat heel and led the way to the entertainment room. The double doors were closed. She glared at Jaren, then knocked lightly. There was no response. Since the woman seemed reluctant, Jaren reached over and knocked on the door herself, harder this time.

The housekeeper gave her a dirty look. A second later, someone inside the room mumbled, "Come in."

The housekeeper turned the knob and opened only one of the doors. It was a mini movie theater, Jaren thought. There were several rows of seats—seven, she counted, with six seats across each row. They sloped down to the *movie screen* which appeared to be some sixty or so inches wide. The ultimate entertainment center. Also good for viewing movies without risking going out.

She had a feeling that Finley had been encouraged to remain on the estate whenever possible.

"I'm sorry, Mr. Finley," the housekeeper apologized, "but Officer Rosetti insisted on seeing you."

"Detective Rosetti," Jaren corrected. The woman merely gave her a condescending look but didn't bother to apologize.

"That's all right, Kathy." Finley, sitting in the first row, rose from his seat. He waved toward the screen. "I was just reminiscing."

Jaren saw what had to be a very old video playing on the screen. Two little boys, carbon copies of one another, were playing in their own private carnival. A handsome man was with them, laughing as he chased after one, then the other. The man bore a strong resemblance to Finley, except that he appeared to be buff and vital, while Finley was fragile and delicate.

Finley aimed his remote control at the screen and it went to black. The lights within the room remained on low as he crossed to her. The housekeeper left, closing the door behind her.

The smile Finley flashed at her might as well have been drawn on for all the feeling behind it. "So, what brings you back, Detective?"

Was it her imagination, or was his voice deeper, more confident than it had been the last time they talked? Jaren cautioned herself not to read into his actions yet.

"There's been another murder, Mr. Massey," she told him. "Same as the others. A stake driven through the heart."

Their gazes locked for a long moment. His eyes looked dead, as if there was nothing beyond the pupils. Eyes were supposed to be the windows to the soul, weren't they? She stifled a shiver that suddenly materialized.

"Why come to me?" he asked her.

Very deliberately, Jaren placed her purse down on the seat closest to her. "I thought that since you were up on vampires, you might have a theory about why these killings were happening."

"Up on vampires?" he echoed. He watched her very carefully now. She was right, she could feel it in her bones. Something about being in the same space as a cold-blooded killer, a stillness in the air, that got to her.

Maybe she should have waited for someone to come with her. "What makes you say that?"

"I read an article about you," she told him, keeping her tone neutral, as if they were just having a conversation. "You and your twin brother were kidnapped as children."

She saw his eyes darken, as if she'd just made a misstep. "I don't want to talk about it."

She pressed on. "In the article I read, you said that vampires kidnapped you. That a vampire was responsible for killing your brother."

Moving away from her, he walked to the front of the theater. "I said I didn't want to talk about it," he insisted, his voice getting higher.

Jaren followed him.

He was unraveling, she thought, nervous excitement telegraphing through her. Just like that. The strain of being on his guard, of being without his father—alone against his enemies—was getting to him, she could almost feel it.

"What are they like?" she asked.

His expression grew almost wild as he cried, "Who?"

"Vampires," she answered matter-of-factly. "Do they look like you and me?"

"I don't know what you're talking about." He covered his ears not to hear any more questions, desperate to get away from her. "I—" Finley stopped, his eyes widening in horror as he saw the book that she was taking out of her purse.

"They don't really look like this, do they?" Jaren pointed to the drawing on the back of the dust jacket. The publisher had a cover artist draw several blood-thirsty-looking creatures, all gathered around a victim, about to feast on him.

Seeing the cover, Finley breathed harder. A look that was close to demonic entered his eyes. It was as if Massey wasn't himself anymore.

For the first time, fear wove through her.

"They won't stop, Derek," Finley wailed, turning to address someone who wasn't in the room. He hardly seemed aware of her at all. "When are they going to stop?" he sobbed.

"Derek," she repeated. He turned full of fury in her direction. She almost had him, she thought. She just needed to have him confess to killing one of the victims, and everything else would fall into place from there. "That was your brother's name, wasn't it? What happened to Derek? Did they kill him, Finley? Did the vampire kill your brother?"

"No," he cried. "No, they didn't kill him. Derek's right here. He fooled them. He came back to me. To protect me now that Dad's gone. Derek protects me," he cried. "Derek protects me. Derek—"

And then, right before her eyes, Finley squared his shoulders and raised his chin. His expression changed, becoming more confident. More in control. When he spoke, his voice was deep.

"Right here, kid. I'm right here. You don't have to be afraid." His eyes shifted to her face. "I'll take care of this one, too, just like I did the others," he promised. "She's not going to hurt you!" he shouted, lunging at her.

Stunned at the transformation she'd just witnessed,

Jaren barely managed to jump back, out of Finley's reach. There was no room for her to turn and draw her weapon. Needing to put some distance between them so she could take charge of the situation, Jaren tried to dart up the small aisle, but Finley, assuming his dead brother's persona, was too fast for her.

Too fast and surprisingly, too strong.

Grabbing her by the legs, he brought her down. Caught off guard, Jaren hit her head against one of the armrests. Hard.

For a moment, a darkness encroached on her, sucking away the light. Threatening to swallow her up. Jaren struggled to keep it at bay, knowing that if she passed out, that would be the end of it. Finley, acting as Derek, would kill her.

"I'm not a vampire, Derek," she cried, struggling to stay conscious. "I'm human. It's all just your imagination."

He didn't seem to hear her. As she struggled to get up, he pinned her down with his weight, straddling her waist. Massey looked around for something to hit her with so that he could finish his work.

"That's what they all said," he jeered. "They said that Finley was crazy because he told them I wasn't dead. Well, he's not crazy and neither am I. And I know what they are. They killed my father and now they want to kill me," he shouted into her face. His eyes glowed as he accused, "You want to kill me."

He was too strong for her. She couldn't knock him off. The more she struggled, the harder he pressed down on her, his knees crushing her ribs.

"No, I don't. I just want to get you help. Your father would want to get you help."

"Don't you talk about him!" he shouted, furious. "Don't you *dare* talk about him, you vampire whore."

"I'm not a vampire," she shouted back. And then she remembered the keepsake she always wore around her neck. "Look, vampires are afraid of crosses. Would I have a cross around my neck if I were a vampire?"

He jerked her closer, holding on to her hair to keep her captive. She could all but feel it ripping out of her head. Disgust filled his voice as he dropped her head with a push. She hit the back of it against the floor. Jaren felt her teeth jar. "You don't have a cross," he shouted back.

"It must have come off in the struggle. But think back," she pleaded. "When I came in, I was wearing one. My dad gave it to me to keep me safe. He was like your dad. Your dad just wanted you to be safe."

Moving his weight farther up so that it centered on her rib cage, Massey doubled up his fists and began pummeling her. The blows made her dizzy.

"Shut up," he screamed, incensed. "Shut up about my father!"

Desperate, her head starting to spin again, Jaren screamed, hoping that the housekeeper was still somewhere close by and would come running in. The woman was protective of him but she couldn't be a party to anything like murder—could she?

No one came. She felt her lip swelling, felt blood entering her mouth.

"The room's soundproof," she heard Massey laugh just before he landed another blow. Pain went shooting through her jaw. "Scream all you want. It won't do you any good."

The next jarring blow made her ears ring. There was pain everywhere, seductive pain that urged her to slip into the shelter of unconsciousness. She fought against it, but she didn't know how much longer she could hold on.

In the distance, above the ringing in her head, she thought she heard a noise.

An explosion.

The next moment, she felt a heavy weight fall on her, almost smothering her. Her lungs felt as if they were going to burst as she struggled to suck in air. For a second, desperation filled her as it felt like a losing battle.

And then the weight was gone.

Someone called her name. The next moment, strong arms lifted her from the floor. The darkness that threatened to absorb her faded, giving way to light that came streaming into the room.

Pain seared along her ribs, preventing her from taking in a full breath.

When she opened her eyes—not realizing that they had been closed—she saw Kyle bending over her.

Was she dead?

Hallucinating?

Was this what it felt like to drift out of your body for the last time?

With almost superhuman effort, she forced out his name. "Kyle?"

"Idiot!" he cried with relief.

It was Kyle all right. "I'm not dead," she concluded, barely speaking above a whisper.

There were more people in the room. She could hear different voices threading into one another, but she couldn't make sense of any of it. The only one she was really aware of was Kyle.

Kyle, holding her in his arms.

She was safe. Relief wove through her.

"What the hell is wrong with you?" Kyle demanded, his voice breaking. "Do you realize what could have happened to you if I hadn't listened to my voice mail?"

She struggled to draw enough air into her lungs to be able to say, "You've got the same rotten bedside manner as Barrett did."

He didn't know whether to shake her or hug her. "And you have the sense of a flea."

She looked at him, a trace of a smile curving her lips. Or at least, she tried to smile. Whether or not she succeeded, she couldn't tell.

"I have enough sense to leave you a voice message," she reminded him. "Finley Massey is insane. He thought he was his dead brother, Derek, and that vampires were after him. He was trying to kill them all in order to protect *Finley*."

Kyle glanced toward the inert body on the floor. Riley was slipping handcuffs on the unconscious man.

"He won't be killing vampires anytime soon," he promised her.

For a moment, all he wanted to do was hold Jaren close to him, to feel her chest rising and falling against his own. Silently, he offered up a prayer of thanksgiving that he had managed to get here when he had, and not ten minutes later.

It was the first time Kyle remembered praying in a very long time.

# Chapter 15

"I don't need to go to the hospital."

Jaren used what felt like the last of her available energy to voice her adamant protest. It fell on deaf ears.

Instead of halting the transport, Kyle merely stood to the side as the paramedics loaded the gurney she was on into the back of one of the two ambulances.

The other took a wounded, unconscious Finley Massey to another hospital.

Kyle gave no indication that he even heard her. It was only once she was inside the ambulance and he had climbed in beside her, that he could examine her.

His eyes, she thought vaguely, looked angry.

"No arguments," he ordered. "Massey used your face for a punching bag."

He had no doubts that the deranged man had done it in order to knock her unconscious so that she could offer no resistance when he drove the stake into her chest.

The very thought made his blood run cold.

"We need to find out if he caused any brain damage— more than you already have," he amended, barely controlling the fear-fueled anger that boiled within him.

Her chest was killing her, but she managed to insist, "I'm fine."

The last thing she remembered before the world suddenly faded to black was Kyle looking at her and saying, "The hell you are, Rosetti. Rosetti? Jaren?"

In the distance, Jaren thought that she heard him urgently calling her name over and over again, but she was too far away to answer.

Kyle hated waiting. For that reason, he avoided surveillance work whenever he could.

But he found himself waiting now.

Waiting while the hospital technicians ran MRIs and lab tests on Jaren. Waiting and restlessly leaning against pastel-colored walls, moving from one to another like a man who didn't belong anywhere.

Waiting to be informed that Jaren was going to be all right despite her stupid stunt. Waiting as he became acutely aware of a feeling gripping him that he had never experienced before.

Concern wasn't anything new for him. He'd been concerned as he became aware of his mother's situation:

a single mother in failing health with three children to raise and care for. He'd always been protective of her and of his brother and sister even though he wasn't the oldest except for a technicality.

It was just the way things were, just the way he was built.

But this time around, something went beyond the concern. There had been a real, bottomless fear that Jaren was in real danger. That she could die before he reached her.

And that if she did, he would never be the same again.

The minute he'd gotten out of court, something—intuition maybe—had made him check his voice mail. As soon as he heard Jaren's voice, he could feel his gut tightening into a knot. He knew before he even listened to the whole message that she was going to go off on her own and do something stupid.

Something dangerous.

Like a man possessed, he'd lost no time tearing out of the courthouse parking lot, steering the vehicle with one hand while hitting numbers on his cell phone's keypad with the other. He pulled a team together for backup before he actually had a reason to believe it was necessary.

Because he *knew.*

Deep down in his gut, he knew Jaren was in trouble. Knew she was right about her hunch that Massey was the killer. And as sure as night followed day, he knew that she was going to be the man's next victim unless he got to her in time.

Driving like a madman, he'd broken out in a cold sweat as he shakily searched his mind for the prayers his mother had taught him as a little boy.

And even now, standing in this antiseptic hospital, the silence of the night echoing back at him, he was far from convinced that the worst was over. Jaren had been pretty badly beaten.

What if—?

His breathing grew short. He couldn't let himself go there. Not yet.

"Knew I'd find you here."

Lost in thought, he shook himself free as he looked up. Kyle saw Riley approaching him. She wasn't alone. Less than a step behind her were Greer and Ethan. Kyle struggled to pull himself together.

And then, as if someone had thrown open the main hospital doors, Brian and Andrew came in just several steps in front of what looked like an avalanche of Cavanaughs. Every last one of them and their spouses had come to lend their moral support.

Andrew reached him first. "How is she, son?" he asked.

Kyle shook his head. It took a second before he said, "They haven't told me yet." Even as the words came out, his throat felt as if it was closing.

"She's a tough girl," Brian told him with an unshakable certainty. "She'll pull through." He smiled at the younger man. "Nice work, by the way, catching Massey."

The praise meant nothing to him. There was a hollowness inside that he didn't know how to get around or what to do with. "Rosetti was the one who solved the case."

Brian merely nodded. He slipped a comforting arm around Kyle's shoulders.

Kyle's first instinct was to shrug the arm off. But he didn't follow through. Instead, he realized that he was actually drawing comfort from the simple gesture.

Maybe this, he told himself silently, was what being part of an extended family was all about. Having someone there who actually cared about what he was going through.

That realization was followed by another. He rather liked having the support. That instead of sucking away his independence, being part of a greater whole actually made him feel stronger.

"I brought food," Andrew announced as Callie, Teri, Rayne and Clay, four of his five children, came in, hefting coolers between them.

"Of course you did," Brian said with a laugh, shaking his head.

"Hey, you have a long vigil ahead of you, it doesn't hurt to have a full stomach," Andrew pointed out.

No one argued. They were all too busy clustering around the coolers, helping themselves to the covered containers that were inside.

Like Andrew said, there was a long vigil ahead of them.

She'd drifted in and out of consciousness several times. Each time, she was acutely aware that there was someone sitting by her bed. But she'd fade away again before she could focus or discover who it was.

Finally, struggling to hold on to consciousness, Jaren forced her eyes open and looked, half expecting that her imagination had conjured up the figure in the chair and there was no one there. After all, who did she know here who felt close enough to her to put in that kind of time, waiting for her to come around?

But when she focused her eyes, the figure didn't fade away. Instead, he took on features.

Kyle.

Looking at her and frowning.

Nothing unusual there.

She wanted to laugh, but couldn't. Her throat felt like rawhide. Had they shoved a tube down it at some point to help her breathe? No, wait, that maniac, Finley, had tried to choke her.

Massey.

Her head began to throb as her memory of the last events returned. But at least she was alive, she thought. And that was something.

A big something.

Kyle was still frowning. And not saying anything. She took in a deep breath, then another, trying to get to the point where she could talk.

It wasn't as easy as she would have liked. But she stubbornly persisted until she heard her voice weakly emerge.

"You're mad at me, aren't you?" she finally managed to ask, breaking the silence. Her voice sounded as if it belonged to a ninety-three-year-old chronic smoker, she thought disparagingly. But at least she could talk.

"Yeah."

The single word hung in the air. Kyle didn't trust himself to say anything else. He'd been here all night, after assuring everyone else that they should go home and that he'd call if there was any change.

Andrew had been the last to go after making him promise that if he needed anything, anything at all, he wouldn't hesitate to call. It was the only way the patriarch could be persuaded to leave the hospital.

Jaren sucked in another long breath. Her lungs ached and it felt as if there was a lead weight on her rib cage. She looked down, knowing that she wouldn't see anything. But it was going to take a while before the image of Massey, straddling her, would leave her in peace.

"But everything turned out all right," she finally said.

"Yeah, but it damn well might not have," Kyle retorted, his hold on stoicism abruptly shattering. His anger almost exploded and only the most extreme control on his part kept it under wraps. "What the hell were you thinking?" he demanded. "You were supposed to wait for me—or at the very least, not go running off like that on your own!"

In hindsight, she knew Kyle was right. But that didn't give him the right to talk down to her. She couldn't stand being treated like anything but the independent, capable woman she felt she was. "I'm not a child, Kyle."

"Then why the hell did you act like one?" he shot back.

Anger gave her strength.

"I was afraid Massey would take off and there wasn't anyone around in the conference room," she answered defensively.

"Did you even *try* to get in contact with anyone?" he demanded heatedly.

Her eyes narrowed and flashed. "I called you," she reminded him.

And thank God for that, he thought. "Besides me," he growled.

"No." She breathed out. Even worked up, she could feel her strength ebbing again. "What are you so angry about? We got him."

Was she serious? Didn't she realize what had almost happened? "I'm angry because if I hadn't gotten there in time, he could have killed you."

Kyle would have probably been happier that way, she thought angrily. "Then we wouldn't be having this argument."

"We wouldn't be having *anything,*" Kyle shot back. He struggled to lower his voice, but wasn't too successful at it. "Damn it, Rosetti, do I have to spell it out for you?"

O'Brien had completely lost her. "Spell what out for me?"

As he spoke, he could feel his heart all but twisting in his chest. "That I couldn't have stood it if something had happened to you."

She shrugged, or tried to. "Don't worry. The Chief of Ds wouldn't have blamed you for losing two people in your group."

He stared at her as if she'd started babbling nonsense. "The hell with blame. The hell with all of it. Can't you understand what I'm saying?"

Her head aching—not to mention that the painkiller was wearing off—Jaren was more lost than ever. "Obviously not."

"I'm in love with you, Rosetti," Kyle all but spat out. It was hard to say which of them was more surprised to hear him utter the words. "I don't know why, but I am. And if anything happened to you—if you let your bull-headedness get you killed—I—"

Words failed him. Kyle threw up his hands in order to keep from sweeping Jaren into his arms and just holding her to him. He knew she was in far too much pain for him to do that.

"I don't know what I would have done," he admitted in a lower voice.

She stared at him, numb. Numb and dumbstruck. Of all the things she'd expected Kyle to say, to vent, that didn't even come close to being one of them.

He loved her?

Since when?

How the hell had that come out? Kyle silently upbraided himself, horrified by what he'd just blurted out without preamble. Since when couldn't he keep his own counsel?

Damn it, he shouldn't have said anything. His feelings were his own business, not anyone else's. Not even hers.

He had absolutely no idea what she felt for him—if anything—and he refused to look or sound like some kind of lovesick fool.

Kyle abruptly rose to his feet. His chair began to fall backward, but he grabbed it in time to keep it from toppling to the floor.

Emotionless, he stared passed her head. "I told the chief I'd call him when you regained consciousness. I'll see you around."

And with that, he left. Before she could say anything.

Kyle heard the doorbell ring just as he was about to sit down to eat the dinner he'd thrown together. The last couple of weeks, he'd been living off the so-called leftovers that Andrew had pressed on him after the former chief of police had swung by "just to talk."

For a second, Kyle thought of ignoring the doorbell, then decided that it would just be simpler to answer it. In the last two weeks, various members of the Cavanaugh family—his family, he silently corrected—had stopped by after hours, seemingly to shoot the breeze.

It was, he knew, their way of showing concern, and even though he acted like he was perfectly happy by himself, he was growing more and more open to their company.

It helped him cope with the emptiness that kept widening within him.

Getting up from the table, he went to the door. He

opened it, but the token greeting on his lips faded to silence. It wasn't one of the Cavanaughs on his doorstep. Or either one of his siblings. It was Jaren, looking a great deal better than she had the last time he'd seen her.

Still somewhat pale, the bruises that had disfigured her delicate face were a thing of the past now. She was as beautiful as ever.

More.

"You never came back to see me." Softly voiced, it was still an accusation.

Caught off guard, Kyle belatedly stepped back to let her enter. "I thought you'd be better off if I—"

How did he end this sentence? he silently wondered. His feelings were something he was going to have to come to terms with. He should have never burdened her with the revelation.

"If you took the coward's way out?" she supplied when his voice trailed off.

Kyle bristled at the portrayal. "I didn't want to make you feel that you were on the spot—that I expected you to answer. Or to return the feeling," he added firmly.

"You never gave me a chance to answer," she retorted heatedly. "It was hard for me to breathe, much less form a complete sentence quickly." Her eyes held his. "I can answer you now."

He remembered her little speech about their lovemaking not meaning anything. He didn't have to hear her formally tell him that she was flattered, but that she just didn't feel the same way about him that he did about her.

"Look, Rosetti—Jaren," he corrected himself, making it more personal. "You don't have to—"

"Shut up, O'Brien," she ordered. And then her expression softened just a little. "Let someone else talk for a second."

"Obviously, I don't have a choice in the matter," he commented, bracing himself. "Go ahead."

Doubling her fist, Jaren caught him by surprise for a second time in as many minutes when she punched him in the arm. He was even more surprised to discover that the blow stung. She was stronger than she looked.

"You big, dumb jerk."

"Nice start."

She gave no indication that she heard him. "You can't tell a woman you're in love with her and then just walk away."

He thought that telling her he hadn't intended on telling her that he loved her, that it had just come out, would only earn him another punch, so he refrained. "I didn't know there were rules."

"Of course there're rules," she cried. "And the rules say that you have to let the woman get a chance to answer you."

It was his own fault. He'd started this. "All right."

"I love you," she told him. "I don't want to, but there you have it. I do."

It took him a moment to recover. Something stirred inside of him. Something he didn't quite recognize at first. Happiness? Was that what this warm feeling in the pit of his stomach was? "Why don't you want to?"

She never thought that she would have to explain herself to a man. Didn't men have a natural phobia when it came to commitment?

"Because love makes you vulnerable. Love leaves you wide open to being abandoned. To being hurt, and I've had enough of that. I don't want to be hurt. Ever again," she said with feeling. And then she took a deep breath, her eyes hopeful. "Can you love me without hurting me, Kyle?" she asked in a softer voice.

He smiled at her. Maybe blurting out that he loved her hadn't been the stupidest thing he'd ever done. "That would be the plan."

"Then don't walk out on me again."

He took her into his arms. "I think I can manage that."

She could feel adrenaline beginning to rush through her veins, as if she'd just taken a dive off the high board and had scored a perfect ten.

"The doctor cleared me," she told him. "You can kiss me. For as long as you want to."

He smiled down at her as he framed her face with his hands. "Nice to know," he murmured as he began to bring his mouth down to hers.

For the third time, Jaren surprised him by placing her fingertips over his lips, stopping him. When he looked at her she said, "But first, tell me again."

He pretended not to understand. "Tell you what?"

"You know."

His mouth curved. Yeah, he knew. "I love you."

She raised herself up on her toes, bringing her mouth closer to his. Her eyes were shining as she told him, "Me, too," just before she kissed him.

And went on to completely lose herself in the safety of his arms. Where she knew she belonged from this day forward.

\* \* \* \* \*

*Don't miss Marie Ferrarella's next romance,*
*THE AGENT'S SECRET BABY*
*available October 2009 from*
*Silhouette Romantic Suspense.*

**We'll be spotlighting a different series
every month throughout 2009
to celebrate our 60th anniversary.**

**Look for Silhouette® Nocturne™ in October!**

Travel through time to experience tales
that reach the boundaries of life and death.
Bestselling authors Lindsay McKenna, Cindy
Dees, P.C. Cast and Merline Lovelace join
together in a brand-new, four-book
Time Raiders miniseries.

# TIME RAIDERS

August—*The Seeker*
by *USA TODAY* bestselling author Lindsay McKenna

September—*The Slayer* by Cindy Dees

October—*The Avenger*
by *New York Times* bestselling author and
coauthor of the House of Night novels P.C. Cast

November—*The Protector*
by *USA TODAY* bestselling author Merline Lovelace

*Available wherever books are sold.*

# You're invited to join our Tell Harlequin Reader Panel!

By joining our new reader panel you will:

- Receive Harlequin® books—they are FREE and yours to keep with no obligation to purchase anything!
- Participate in fun online surveys
- Exchange opinions and ideas with women just like you
- Have a say in our new book ideas and help us publish the best in women's fiction

*In addition, you will have a chance to win great prizes and receive special gifts! See Web site for details. Some conditions apply. Space is limited.*

To join, visit us at

**www.TellHarlequin.com.**

THBPA0108

In 2009 Harlequin celebrates
60 years of pure reading pleasure!

We're marking this occasion by offering
16 **FREE** full books to download and read.

Visit

# www.HarlequinCelebrates.com

to choose from a variety of
great romance stories
that are absolutely **FREE!**

(Total approximate retail value of $60)

We invite you to visit and share the Web site
with your friends, family
and anyone who enjoys reading.

# SPECIAL EDITION

### FROM *NEW YORK TIMES* BESTSELLING AUTHOR

# SUSAN MALLERY

## THE SHEIK AND THE BOUGHT BRIDE

Victoria McCallan works in Prince Kateb's palace. When Victoria's gambling father is caught cheating at cards with the prince, Victoria saves her father from going to jail by being Kateb's mistress for six months. But the darkly handsome desert sheik isn't as harsh as Victoria thinks he is, and Kateb finds himself attracted to his new mistress. But Kateb has already loved and lost once—is he willing to give love another try?

*Available in October wherever books are sold.*

SSE65481

# REQUEST YOUR FREE BOOKS!

## 2 FREE NOVELS PLUS 2 FREE GIFTS!

*Silhouette*® Romantic

# SUSPENSE

### Sparked by Danger, Fueled by Passion!

**YES!** Please send me 2 FREE Silhouette® Romantic Suspense novels and my 2 FREE gifts (gifts are worth about $10). After receiving them, if I don't wish to receive any more books, I can return the shipping statement marked "cancel." If I don't cancel, I will receive 4 brand-new novels every month and be billed just $4.24 per book in the U.S. or $4.99 per book in Canada. That's a savings of at least 15% off the cover price! It's quite a bargain! Shipping and handling is just 50¢ per book*. I understand that accepting the 2 free books and gifts places me under no obligation to buy anything. I can always return a shipment and cancel at any time. Even if I never buy another book from Silhouette, the two free books and gifts are mine to keep forever.

240 SDN EYL4 340 SDN EYMG

| | | |
|---|---|---|
| Name | (PLEASE PRINT) | |
| Address | | Apt. # |
| City | State/Prov. | Zip/Postal Code |

Signature (if under 18, a parent or guardian must sign)

### Mail to the Silhouette Reader Service:
**IN U.S.A.:** P.O. Box 1867, Buffalo, NY 14240-1867
**IN CANADA:** P.O. Box 609, Fort Erie, Ontario L2A 5X3

Not valid to current subscribers of Silhouette Romantic Suspense books.

**Want to try two free books from another line?**
**Call 1-800-873-8635 or visit www.morefreebooks.com.**

* Terms and prices subject to change without notice. Prices do not include applicable taxes. Sales tax applicable in N.Y. Canadian residents will be charged applicable provincial taxes and GST. Offer not valid in Quebec. This offer is limited to one order per household. All orders subject to approval. Credit or debit balances in a customer's account(s) may be offset by any other outstanding balance owed by or to the customer. Please allow 4 to 6 weeks for delivery. Offer available while quantities last.

**Your Privacy:** Silhouette is committed to protecting your privacy. Our Privacy Policy is available online at www.eHarlequin.com or upon request from the Reader Service. From time to time we make our lists of customers available to reputable third parties who may have a product or service of interest to you. If you would prefer we not share your name and address, please check here. ☐

SRS09R

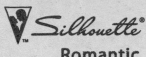

## Romantic SUSPENSE

**Sparked by Danger, Fueled by Passion.**

# *The Agent's Secret Baby*

### by *USA TODAY* bestselling author

# Marie Ferrarella

## TOP SECRET DELIVERIES

Dr. Eve Walters suddenly finds herself pregnant
after a regrettable one-night stand and turns to an
online chat room for support. She eventually learns
the true identity of her one-night stand: a DEA agent
with a deadly secret. Adam Serrano does not want
this baby or a relationship, but can fear for Eve's
and the baby's lives convince him that this is what
he has been searching for after all?

### *Available October wherever books are sold.*

**Look for upcoming titles in
the TOP SECRET DELIVERIES miniseries**

*The Cowboy's Secret Twins* by Carla Cassidy—November
*The Soldier's Secret Daughter* by Cindy Dees—December

**Visit Silhouette Books at www.eHarlequin.com**

Romantic
# SUSPENSE

## COMING NEXT MONTH

### Available September 29, 2009

**#1579 PASSION TO DIE FOR—Marilyn Pappano**
It's Halloween in Copper Lake, and someone's playing tricks. When Ellie Chase's estranged mother is murdered, all the evidence points to her. Ex-boyfriend and detective Tommy Maricci believes she's innocent, and will do anything to prove it. But Ellie has secrets in her past, and she can't remember what she did that night. Could she be guilty?

**#1580 THE AGENT'S SECRET BABY—Marie Ferrarella**
*Top Secret Deliveries*
Eve Walters's affair abruptly ended when she discovered her lover was actually a drug dealer. Now, eight months later, she's pregnant with his child when Adam Serrano walks back into her life—sending her into labor! An undercover DEA agent, Adam is bound to protect Eve and their child from the criminals he's trying to catch. But who will protect his heart from falling for his new family?

**#1581 THE CHRISTMAS STRANGER—Beth Cornelison**
*The Bancroft Brides*
Trying to move forward with her life, widow Holly Bancroft Cole still wants answers about her husband's murder. When she hires sexy but secretive Matt Rankin to finish the renovations on her farmhouse for Christmas, she never expects him to heal her heart. Except Matt is more closely connected to Holly's past than either of them know—and once revealed, it could destroy their second chance at love.

**#1582 COLD CASE AFFAIR—Loreth Anne White**
*Wild Country*
When pregnant Manhattan journalist Muirinn O'Donnell is forced to return to her small Alaskan hometown, she slams right into the past she's tried so hard to forget. Jett Rutledge doesn't want to see her either. They both have secrets to keep, but as Muirinn investigates a twenty-year-old mystery, danger sends her back into Jett's protective arms....

SRSCNMBPA0909